THE SMUGGLERS

VANESSA MACLAREN-WRAY

Published by Water Dragon Publishing
waterdragonpublishing.com

An imprint of Paper Angel Press
paperangelpress.com

ISBN 978-1-957146-61-4

FIRST EDITION

10 9 8 7 6 5 4 3 2 1

For children who choose to be themselves, and for their parents.
You know who you are.

THE SMUGGLERS

1

SEPARATION

T HE DEPARTING SKIP-SHIP dwindled slowly on the viewscreen. Boy kept all seven eyes focused there, holding fast to his attachment with Papa. Moment by moment, their connection stretched to a wire as fine as a quantum string. He knew his father was holding tight at the other end. He could feel the bright glimmer that was distinctively Papa, and only Papa, shining like a guidepost in his mind. When the ship reached its transfer point, and flashed into the skip-stream, the glimmer vanished.

Behind him, Mother cried out — a sharp cry like talons tearing through steel.

He waited, eyes still fixed on the quiet viewscreen, but no such pain struck him. Instead, a fluttering of memory unspooled in his mind. The calm, confident touch of Papa's fronds, and the way they could extend the length of their ship's bridge or curl tight and protective around a troubled child. The sensation of flight as Papa flung him high in the empty cargo bay, spinning and laughing, dizzy with the joy of flight. The silvery-grey featherings that concealed Papa's tools, his talons, his wise and delicate fingers. The warm brush of his fluff, when he let Boy ride atop his carapace, hunkered down, pretending they raced through the crystalline forests of Darrougha, in pursuit of dangerous prey. His voice, chittering nothings at the creatures they transported, the wild, unique beasts he loved so well.

Not so well as he loved Boy. Or Mother. Or, now, that other for whom he'd left them all.

Everyone changes, Mother said. Always, Papa had been the same, but he left with a new voice, with stripes of amber in his feathers, a sharper, more abrupt way of moving his fronds, and a quicker beat to his walk, his feet striking the deck in a new rhythm. Boy hadn't known his father before, when Papa had been female. He'd changed then, for Mother.

Now, Papa had changed again, for someone else.

When will I change?

Papa said he got his name from his father.

Who will name me, now, when I find my own self?

"Mama?" He turned away from the viewscreen, to find Mother curled in a tight ball. Her featherings twitched and a low drone rumbled from her voicebox. He scuttled to her side and spread his fronds around her. "Mama? Are you all right? What's the matter?"

She uncurled one frond and wrapped it around him. The trembling of it vibrated through him. His hearts beat out of rhythm.

"Mama?"

"I will be all right, Boy. I couldn't make myself let go until the very last." Her frond brushed over his fluff, teasing his eyes into retracting down safe. "Are you all right, my dear?"

"I'm fine, Mama. Why would I not be all right?"

A whisper of silver-grey flickered in his memory, then faded out of reach. The bridge of their skip-ship seemed too large. Something was missing. No, *someone* was missing. Someone important to the family business.

"Good, then. Not to worry. How about you go feed our merchandise and then do your studying?"

Mama did not look well, he decided. "I'll feed the cretzina, Mama, but then I'll bring you something." His balance felt wrong, as if he'd just been doing cartwheels in the cargo bay. "I don't think I can study right now. I'm worried about you."

She patted his carapace and her fronds relaxed, but he could tell she was doing it on purpose. "Don't worry, dear. It's been a difficult day is all. Tomorrow will be better."

"Tomorrow?"

"Yes, tomorrow we will jump into the skip-stream ourselves and set course for the station. The Truck Stop, this one is called."

"Why?"

She pulled her fronds back around her and mumbled, "Not now, Boy, not now."

•   •   •

Deralka watched her child as he skittered from the bridge, intent on his tasks, his questions held back for now. She had questions of her own, mostly about how she would carry out this last operation with Boy as her partner. Their specialized business, delivering much-desired prizes to persons of means, had relied on two adults capable of technique and guile, sharing the work in all its exquisite detail. They'd never once been apprehended, never failed in a delivery, never lost a precious beast. The arrangements this time had involved negotiating with dangerous predators in human shape — the secretive criminal organization that owned the fabled station. While the laws at the Truck Stop might be more forgiving than elsewhere, there were worse dangers than the law. Should humans become aware that Darroughons stalked their passageways, there could not be a good end for any of them. She might get away with smuggling the cretzina, but fail at securing her own self. Or her child.

She'd been worried about Boy. He had reached that age when children begin to mature, to form adult attachments — ones that should be lifelong, like the one she had just severed. *He'll be fine, it's easier for children.* Then again, stress accelerates maturation, and no one could say the past few weeks had not been stressful. She had shielded him as best she could, but she couldn't protect him from everything. Her mate's change seemed to have troubled him more than the departure. Perhaps he worried about his own changes, but didn't want to ask her.

He should talk to his father, she thought. Then clenched her fronds tightly around herself, sheltering the ache that seemed to come from everywhere but her mind. The daggers of her talons extended, ready for battle, as if she crouched in the ancient forest, prepared to defeat and devour her enemies.

The ship would fly itself for now. Though Deralka was the better pilot, her mate had excelled at programming the auto systems, and she-that-had-been-him had taken extra care to check and re-check those settings before she left.

I'll need to study those manuals, now. Perhaps Boy would like to learn alongside me.

Thinking helped to manage her feelings. It had always been that way. He-that-was-now-she had used feelings more, applied intuitions to guide thinking. Perhaps that was why the bond with Boy had been so strong. Deralka had watched the gleam of their attachment, expecting it to fail at boarding the shuttle, at reaching the other ship. Instead, it persisted right up to the point the other ship skipped free of the here-and-now.

She forced herself to think through the next stages in their journey: the job left to be done, the repayment of their debts, their escape to a place of safety.

Moment by moment, the fire in her joints eased to an ache, her fronds relaxed, her heartbeats steadied. When Boy returned carrying a tray laden with his favorite snacks and a full — and, for once, properly-sealed — flask of water, she found herself able to taste a few morsels and drink down all the water. His quietness disturbed her — Boy was never inclined to sit still — but her own behavior would likely have frightened him.

"Don't worry about me, dear," she reassured him. "I'll be quite all right by tomorrow."

She wanted to ask Boy what he remembered, but that could be counterproductive. Children were meant to part from their parents, to form new attachments. It was part of the natural order, though nature did not design for skip-ship velocities of separation.

"Tell me, Mama —" He seemed to change his mind about what he wanted to ask. His fronds twitched as he reached for an alternate question. "Tell me about the station. Why is it called that?"

"The Truck Stop? It's an old human phrase from when they would sail around on their oceans. A truck is a special piece at the top of the mast that the sails connect to."

"Humans had sailing ships, too?"

"It's not that uncommon for water worlds." She rasped a laugh, surprising herself. "I see you have been skipping some of your lessons. What if we settle on a water world?"

He opened another packet of snacks and pushed most of them across the tray towards her. "I didn't skip lessons, Mama. I just didn't pay attention. I'll do better."

She took a few of the crunchy dried arthropods and lifted her eyes to study him better. It wasn't like Boy to admit such things.

"So a truck stop is a place where ships stop?" he asked.

"Yes, it's a place where the skip-ships stop — ones like ours and the big transports — for fuel and rest and recreation. The truck stop name doesn't quite make sense, because the truck is such a small part of a sailing ship. Perhaps, when we visit, you can ask someone about it."

He perked up at the idea. "Yes. I'll do that. We're supposed to be tourists, right, Mama? And tourists ask lots of questions." He crunched a few treats. "*Are* we going to a water world?"

"We'll see, we'll see. Once we complete this last transaction, we'll have our stake, we can make that choice together." All those plans she'd made with Boy's father, she set aside. They'd narrowed their choices to a few worlds, but she knew each of them would remind her of what she'd lost. *I'll need to begin anew.* For the first time in many years, she regretted cutting all her attachments on Darrougha. Then again, could Boy ever be content with one world, however beautiful, when he'd seen so many places in his short life?

"All right."

He seemed as lost in thought as she was, fiddling with the snacks on the tray. He set two of the many-legged morsels against one another in a duel to destruction. The one that snapped in two first earned a quicker passage to his stomach.

"Don't play with your food," she admonished, but she couldn't conceal the buzz of laughter his antics inspired in her.

Boy made his voice deep and grumbly. "I'm not playing, I'm practicing for when we settle on the World of Crunchy Insects!"

"I'll keep that in mind." She pulled another sack open and selected two candidates for herself. "So. How do they battle? Does one have right of first strike? Are their weapons mass or speed?"

The meal not only satisfied their hunger, but also gave them many little tasks to complete afterwards, with bits of insect armor and fragments of flavored coatings scattered into the most unlikely crevices in the bridge stations.

•　　•　　•

For the final approach run, Boy chose the widest of the viewscreens and stretched one pair of his fronds around the perimeter, taking possession of the wonderful sight. The tingling of etheric energy flowing through the conduits that served the sensor arrays added an edge to his excitement. Mama had installed these ancient-tech devices a year ago, and they still surprised him with new capabilities. This time, they could watch every moment of their flight into the galactic core.

"So many stars! Mama, have they put all the stars in the galaxy here?"

Mother laughed at the joke, and his featherings rippled with joy. She stood at the controls, guiding the processes that controlled the ship. She'd told Boy she planned a route that would make the journey worth their while. It was a once-in-a-lifetime experience, arriving at this vast ocean of radiation and gravity.

The flicker of data across the top of the panel let him know just how much the shielding had to screen the light, dimming what must be an impossibly brilliant sky if one dared to look with natural eyes. Thousands of stars — no, millions — danced in their orbits. They all seemed so close to one another, he expected at any moment to see the flare of a stellar collision. He flicked a finger over the controls, triggering layers in the display that tagged each star by type, age, mass, velocity, and luminosity. By extending all his eyes, he could sample all the flavors of starlight, from deep ultraviolets to brilliant infrareds. The layers of color blended to a swirling sea of energy.

"It's like a snowstorm! A storm of light, like on Calivax! Remember, Mama?"

She made a low hum of agreement, then called out, "Shields?"

Boy already had one eye on the shield monitors. Mother had promised they'd be safe, but something told him there should be more than one person keeping watch on their safety.

"Shields holding!" he reported, feeling more grown-up than ever before.

The lower half of the monitor filled with a glowing red-orange disk.

"Look," he cried. "It's an ocean in space!"

"The accretion disk, yes," she replied.

"I know," he grumbled. He'd studied that portion of his lessons thoroughly. At the center of that immense platter lay the black hole itself. "The reason this is a safe place for the station is that this black hole spins slowly, so it doesn't make jets like other galactic black holes."

"Oh, is that so?" This time, he heard the spark-like clatter of pride in her voice. "Now, look, do you see the station?"

He added the filter for reflective objects. Yes. There it was, silhouetted against the glow of the accretion disk: two rings, one tucked inside the other, spokes running straight from the hub to the outermost ring, the whole spinning against the backdrop of the accretion disk's glow. No, wait, there was a third, narrow ring at the rim.

"Is that where we dock? On the outer ring?"

"Yes, that's right. Better go get your skinsuit out, Boy. We'll be there soon."

He tore his gaze from the wonderful view, but not before checking to be sure the viewscreen was recording.

"Mama? Did you remember to install the devices in the skinsuits?"

She murmured a yes, and flicked her fronds at him in approving dismissal. Humans used electronic devices implanted in their skin, mostly to communicate. Darroughon technology made those devices more powerful, but the humans would never know. Boy loved that feeling, holding a secret in plain sight.

He ran to the lockers and pulled out the skinsuits. The big one looked like a human woman, with plain unfeathered copper-brown skin and long hair that flowed like an amber waterfall when Mama walked around in it. The little one had short, black, hair with no curliness to it, and wide, innocent eyes that he could look through with his real eyes, to see far more than any human child could see. He had fun wearing it, but it was getting to be too small.

Never mind. Mama says this is the last time we'll use them.

2

DISEMBARKATION

DERALKA SET BOY to lead the way down their ship's ramp, while she spied out the watchful eyes of monitors in the primary offloading passage. A dynamo of distraction, Boy skipped along, calling out with delight at each step, each new discovery. At the turn to the final disembarkation passage, he paused and waited for her. Pride ruffled her feathers. He'd remembered that part of her plan. Next, they needed to confirm the details their informant had given.

Lights flickered erratically from around the corner. She breathed again. Their hard-won intel had been correct: Docking Bay 43 of the infamous Truck Stop station had technical issues. At least it was no more than faulty lighting circuits. The station maintained its steady spin, yielding a moderate artificial gravity. Deralka guessed her weight at nearly two-thirds of what it would be on Darrougha.

She paused to check the seals along her skinsuit's abdomen and found one irregularity. She smoothed it away with a quick, casual motion of one synthetic human hand. For the benefit of any hidden monitors, she also rubbed her skinsuit's back and made noises matching a human in some moderate discomfort. Beneath the false overskin, the merchandise stirred sleepily, its sheathed feet skittering across the hidden surface of her primary skinsuit. Insurance would cover any damage.

"Have patience, Boy. Nearly there."

"Yes, Mama."

She kept a steady pace down the hatchway ramp, but her mind wandered. This should have been a family trip, an adventure for the three of them together. Now, she had only herself and Boy — and their savings and debts from years of effort. Tomorrow, the mission would be complete, and she could begin to think of the next steps in their journey.

Soon enough, she and Boy would make their way back to Darrougha, for a little while. Her debtors would be waiting, talons extended, but she would fill them with recompense, satisfy their every demand.

They would make themselves free, she and Boy, to be alone but together.

Then, they would seek a home.

Tomorrow, they would gain the means.

Today, they needed food and shelter.

At the foot of the ramp, she stopped in the demarcated area, but still within the arc of shadow cast by the faulty lighting system. She allowed Boy to bounce a little, to fill the space in his lively way. The waiting inspector, a humanoid android, hesitated, focusing on Boy, as Deralka had intended, while taking that one necessary step towards her. He lifted the scanner remote by just that much, to forestall any risk that Boy might interfere with it.

"Purpose of your visit."

The delivery came flat, no intonation. This was surprising. She'd heard a great deal of the Truck Stop's sophisticated androids.

"Refueling. Respite stay." She studied his face as he spoke, and found its complexity of expression failed to match human parameters.

So, it was an android, but a lower-tier one, probably not even sentient. She'd rehearsed many useful lines of conversation, but held her peace. Those clever bits of patter would be useless here.

"Length of stay."

"Two days, estimated." She selected a simple line from her patter. "Can you recommend a good place to stay?" She patted the mound of simulated flesh that curved under her smock like a stolen fuel canister. "A family-friendly place?"

"Obtain recommendations at the kiosk."

At least the android was enabled to respond to selected keywords. Still, how disappointing. She had prepared so well.

It continued with the scan seamlessly, its instrument's path disrupted just enough to blur its view of the merchandise. She waited, measuring the progress of the scan by the indicators so conveniently displayed on its surface. Just as the android finished and began to speak, she interrupted.

"Where is the kiosk?"

The question could not be a true distraction, but the information would be helpful, and she hoped to avoid any delay after the next verbal exchange.

"The kiosk is at the gateway. See the map."

One never knew where and when a conflict situation might arise, so she tapped her wrist, bringing up local options in her heads-up display. Her device had, indeed, automatically absorbed the local map into its database.

"I see. Thank you." Was she free to go now?

"What is this irregularity?" It pointed to her abdomen and tapped the scanner with mechanical menace.

"It's my baby."

She patted the mound, pushing just a little harder where she knew the underlying shape had a protrusion. The merchandise stirred, and a rounded lump appeared at one side of the false skin, gliding under the surface to disappear at the opposite side.

"Oh, look," she said. "He's kicking. Do you want to feel it?" She put on a basic smile, painted lips curving over a closed mouth, knowing the android wouldn't discern it from a more complex smile.

"That will not be necessary." An interesting flow of expressions passed over the android's face, as it sorted through appropriate responses. The resulting thin smile showed a row of perfectly-aligned, never-used teeth.

Deralka toyed with showing him her own teeth, but refrained. "May we proceed?"

"Proceed."

The promised kiosk offered a variety of access panels, accommodating a corresponding diversity of travelers one might encounter at the truck stop. The queue for humanoid-types was the longest, as expected. What she'd not anticipated was the generosity extended to her. On Darrougha, waiting patiently would be considered offensively patronizing.

Here, however, other customers offered to yield their places to her, each for their own reasons. The Oannder turned an unusually deep shade of orange, and confessed a concern that she might deliver the merchandise directly to the deck, disgusting everyone with the profound explicitness of human birth.

A little old Verdia fixed her violet eyes on Boy, gave him a dozen rapid click-smiles, and babbled nonstop. "Oooh, what a pretty little precious you are, my dear. I should open up my bag right now and give you a present. Would you like a little present, my dear? My, my, you are such a sweetie! Wouldn't I like to eat you up right now! But maybe you'd rather go ahead so you can run to buy sweets for yourself at the gift shop? Go, go, such a darling, good, good boy you are!"

Boy kept tight hold of Deralka's hand and responded with wide, seemingly-frightened eyes. Was he really frightened? *Let us out of these suits, and we'll see who eats who,* she thought.

They moved forward in the queue, encouraged by the next visitor, and then the next.

The last person — that is, the first in line — stepped aside wordlessly, his heavy-lidded human eyes examining her and Boy with precise interest.

Within the security of her skinsuit, Deralka's featherings twitched with warning. She made her reservation quickly, glad she had selected a hostel beforehand. The man beside her wore the most banal of dockside attire, could have passed for any worker on liberty, but he was human, and she'd trained herself to read their expressions. This one's face betrayed nothing as he said, "Please, madam, I am in no hurry." Suspicious. Very suspicious.

Within the skinsuit, she paired a high-resolution eye with her infrared one. The added visual input confirmed her first impression. The stiffness in his shoulders, the warm lump of plastic in the pocket hidden under his jacket, the excessive shine of his shoes all spoke loudly of a certain kind of human. One obsessed with laws and regulations.

The moment her device pinged her reservation confirmation and receipt of associated directives, she twirled from the console and murmured her gratitude to each of those who had let her pass.

The man who belonged in a uniform said, "Have a nice visit to our station."

•　　•　　•

Boy wondered when the fun could begin. He'd been promised a fun day, and so far it had all been staying quiet, operating his skinsuit as Mother had asked. He couldn't put too much energy into his movements, to avoid getting any excitement out of the game. He had just about run out of patience. The worst part had been that Verdian who put her face right up to all his visual sensors and showed her shiny flat teeth and declared she had half a mind to eat him. It had made him so ... hungry.

He hoped Mother knew just how much he needed a reward.

He didn't like the way Mother pulled him along by the arm of his skinsuit.

I'm not a baby.

His biting teeth ground together, making a soft noise rumble through his skinsuit like the insides of a hungry human.

When Mother stopped at the elevator bank, he tugged his arm free and wriggled his fronds inside their channels. He wanted to message her with his complaints, but he'd been warned to keep his device quiet until she could silence any spies in the vicinity.

Her musical human voice spoke into his imitation ears, but he could hear her own voice underneath, in its familiar clickety whisper. "We have our place to stay, my dear. The luggagers will deliver our case to the hostel. Now, it is your turn. Where should you like to go first?"

His hearts leapt, a little. He knew what she wanted him to say. She'd talked so many times of the truck stop's famous Observation Room, overlooking the black hole.

Just imagine, we'll be able to see the event horizon, the very edge of the known universe!

But then, he knew, she would stand there, just watching the pretty view and talking about he-who-had-departed, and it would be an hour of nothing but standing in the dark.

It's my turn to choose.

She seemed to read his mind. "It's all right. You may choose what you like and do what you like, now."

"Gift shop! Gift shop! Gift shop!" Boy bounced and leapt and ran circles around her, showing off his agility in the skinsuit, despite its already becoming too small. He flashed his device and shared the route with her, from the offboarding deck on the outer rim to the main ring, where they'd find the Grand Mall and his hearts' desire.

She laughed along with him, but he could tell her mind had drifted elsewhere. He followed her glance to the kiosk. The man back there, the one with the funny shoes, he was pretending not to look at them, but Boy recognized what he was, now that his annoyance with the child-eater was gone. Mother had her eye on the law-man. Boy hoped the law-man liked shopping, because that would be all he'd get to see as he spied his way after them.

The Starchaser Gift Shop presented endless wonders to Boy's eyes, layer on layer of delights to feed the most glorious joy the moment they crossed the threshold. The place was crammed with treasures from spinward to antispinward, inboard to outboard. Boy bounced, ecstatic, down and up the aisles.

He surveyed one aisle, then another, itemizing every potential purchase. The silly magnetic shoes, useful in the lower gravity down in the Habitat Ring, clattered as he ran.

"How many things may I have?"

"Better to ask how much you would spend," Mother advised. "But if you choose wisely, you may have two things. And after, you will have one thing that I have chosen already."

Two things! Something fun for right away, and something complicated for later.

"I'll be very wise, Mama." He set his device to calculating sums of costs of the items he'd tagged so far. "What is the after thing?"

"It is a delicacy that humans have brought from the far reaches of the galaxy. It is called *iced cream*."

"Ice cream," came a correction from behind her. The shopkeeper, a humanoid android wearing a boldly-striped uniform, looked down at Boy with a proper human smile, nearly as perfect as Mother could do. "You will like the ice cream at Burnaby Cool's." Then he sighted the bulge over Mother's abdomen, where their own merchandise was hidden. "Oh, my, may I ask, when are you due?"

"Very soon. One never knows, though, does one?"

His mother seemed pleased. The android at the gate had been boring. This one had complicated speech patterns, almost like a real person. Maybe he was a real person. Who could tell with androids?

"That's a fact. But I admire your boldness to travel this far when so far along." The way he smiled became different. Part of his remark seemed to be humorous.

She smiled in return and started chatting, using phrases that Boy had heard her practicing during their flight. Mother liked the play-acting part of their work, even more than taking care of the animals. Boy left them talking while he explored the rest of the aisles and winnowed his choices down to two: a toy version of an animal from a distant planet called Earth, plus a big box full of rattling parts that promised they could be assembled to make a complete model of the Truck Stop itself. He could spend all of their next flight building the model, and it would be the centerpiece in their new home — the one they'd go to once they cashed out their earnings this time.

I will make Mama proud and help her make our new home beautiful.

The shopkeeper bundled both items into a special carrying bag. He said the bag was a special bonus souvenir, and it was true — one side of the bag held a vivid picture of the truck stop itself and the other side had a picture of the black hole, or rather, its brilliantly-colored accretion disk.

As they left the gift shop, Boy had fun with the swirling effect of turning with the rotation of the station, to head downspin. Meanwhile, he watched his mother watch the lawman being far too obvious, pretending to study the scrolling display at the front of the big casino.

I wonder if he likes iced cream?

The Far-Rim treat was all that had been promised. Boy quickly mastered the technique, to spoon the concoction just so, letting it slip properly through the skinsuit to reach the mouth best suited for sugary treats. He used his device to study the nutrients list, and found that ice cream also contained plenty of protein and good fats and even antioxidants, so it would be healthy as well. The one unfair thing was that others in the shop used their own body parts to slurp ice cream from papery sugar-wafer containers. He wished he could do that, but the skinsuit was too much in the way.

"Mama, I want to lick my ice cream."

"Later, perhaps," she said. "Later. Shall we purchase another serving to take to our quarters?"

"Yes, Mama. Thank you, Mama."

Despite his inner wishes, Boy knew full well that the others in the ice cream shop would not be happy to see any of Boy's tongues, let alone his teeth or claws. They wouldn't even like his raspy, rumbly voice, even though he could make their language sounds perfectly well without the skinsuit's hardware.

It's not fair. I've never hurt a human. No one in my family ever ate even one of them.

The law-man didn't come into the shop, but Boy saw him as they were leaving, each carrying a small bag — with small renditions of the Truck Stop and the black hole — containing iced cream packed into a cold-preserving box. He wanted to taunt the law-man, to play a trick on him with iced cream and artificial gravity and the slippery swirl of rotational forces, but Boy knew the importance of this visit. Mother had promised this would be their last sale, that afterwards, they would find a safe place, and settle down together. He would not endanger that, not for anything, not even for the best of fun.

3

NOT THE RESORT HOTEL

DERALKA HAD SELECTED a hostel close by the exotic Resort Hotel, where elaborately-costumed travelers of many species wandered freely through softly-sighing entry doors. It did not escape her attention that a certain law-man strolled by, pretending to be intent on investigating the hotel's ambiance. She skirted the glow of the Resort's energy-wasting lights, to the hostel's entry, thrown into shadow by its neighbor's excesses. Boy's boots clunked along beside her, keeping him firmly attached to the floor of this low-gravity environment.

The hostel proprietor proved to be a living human, not an android. As he verified their registration for a private room, she tried to engage him in small talk about androids. Apparently, the prevalence of android workers was the doing of the Founders, it was insufferable, the Syndicate had a chokehold on the supply, and how was one to compete when one's neighbors had so very many of those androids? It was all the fault of a Mister Khlahth and a Mister Ultich, who held stock in most of the hospitality businesses, not to mention the casino.

"Someone should have stuffed both of them into a driveless hulk and pushed it into the black hole years ago!" he ranted.

Once started, their host never stopped talking.

"Look, there, the luggagers, they have a monopoly on those!" The little baggage-delivery robot surrendered their humble overnight bags, without complaint.

"Come along, come along, best use the elevator, given you've got those heavy bags."

The elevator was a tight fit for the three of them plus the luggage.

"I'd never afford the site fees without those researchers always coming to poke around in the Orange Quadrant down here."

Their host had a great many unverifiable opinions about what might or might not be going on in that sector, though Deralka managed to glean one probably-true tidbit: that Habitat Ring's Orange Quadrant had no active connection to its counterpart in the Main Ring. "You'll never see *that* elevator running, mark my words!"

Why she would want to watch an elevator, that was beyond her.

"Here now, where's your devices? Let's get your access key encoded. Oh, fancy are we? All the fancy people have those built-in ones now. What's wrong with a nice, reliable wristband device?"

She closed the door on him, deeply regretting asking that one question. She'd not gained any better understanding of the various types of automatons on the station. To whom did they report? To the man with the shiny shoes who seemed to like ice cream and gift shops and following ladies to their hostels? To the Messers Khlahth and Ultich, who might have been criminals, or might simply have been better businessmen than her host? To the mysterious Founders, whoever or wherever they might be?

Only the third possibility gave her any comfort.

She sealed the door, then checked the Emergency Safety Card.

"Come here, my dear, you need to read this, too."

Boy set down his packages and patiently listened to her lecture on the importance of safety protocols in a strange spacecraft. He took the safety card himself and read it out loud while she performed a thorough scan of the room for any hidden spies. She found one, but it was a simple type intended to skim account data from a visitor's device.

In short order, she trained her device to feed the little spybot a steady stream of random numbers.

Boy placed the safety card back in its spot and said, "Now, Mama?" His hands were at his throat, ready.

"Yes, dear." She resonated with agreement, all too ready to relax. "Be careful, you'll need that tomorrow, and we have promised to return it undamaged."

"Yes, Mama."

She watched and listened as Boy unsealed his skinsuit and wriggled free of the contraption, spreading his fronds to their full length and shaking out all the joints. He was right, that suit had become far too small for comfort.

We'll buy a new one as soon as the funds clear.

Despite his eagerness, he took due care with the suit, as he'd been taught. She heard no sounds of tearing or of any strain on seals or connections. The moment his little feet struck the floor, he began to struggle with folding the skinsuit.

She went to his aid, showing him the interior marks that indicated predesigned fold points that made the job much easier.

"Well done, Boy. Well done."

In that configuration, the suit fit tidily into the cupboard provided for clothing.

"Thank you, Mama. Your turn. I'll come help as soon as you need me."

Filled with pride and politeness, he took his gift shop bag to the opposite corner and sat to unpack his prizes. The small item, a printed model of some sort of alien animal with a long tail and big ears, soon danced and yipped atop the still-sealed box of the large item.

First things first. She could not undress without removing the surface protecting the merchandise. The larger of their bags yielded up the package labeled "Baby Bed", which she quickly assembled to a tidy enclosure for the creature. The seeming insulation from the hard case soon reverted to its proper role as comfortable bedding in the enclosure.

"It's time, Boy."

Immediately, he let go of the toy, leaving it to dance and yip in solitude. "How can I help, Mama?"

"Well now, with luck it will be asleep, but with animals, one never knows, does one? If it wakes, will you catch it for me? It will not be so afraid of you, as you are closer to its size. Put your big teeth away, my dear."

All his eyes glittered, and he bobbed his head, locking down his biting jaw, so as not to seem threatening to the little creature.

"All right then."

Boy positioned himself close at hand, all four of his real legs spread low and balanced, his fronds spread to catch the beast gently if it made a dash for it. With practiced skill, she manipulated the human fingers of her skinsuit to break the seal on the panel that had carried the merchandise all the long day. Its smell wafted up.

"Not long, now, little one," she murmured.

The upper-edge seal released fully in moments. She sat on the edge of the bed to unlatch the connection points to the lower-edge seal, then leaned back to support the mass of creature and container as she ran her fingers along the lower edge, right, then left. She rotated the domed object just slightly, enough to be sure it was completely free. Then, in one swift motion, she tipped the whole skinsuit back to its standing position, rocking the dome downwards as she did, so that in the end it formed a neat little bed for the sleeping creature.

Boy extended his legs, so he could peer over the edge. The cretzina's fluffy white coat, formed of masses of featherlike hairs, ruffled as it breathed air through its spiracles. Its cute little legs, striped in a dozen brilliant hues, churned as if it dreamed of scuttling along in its native forests.

"Oooh," Boy breathed.

The cretzina's antennae rose up, each lifting an eye to survey its world.

Then it leapt.

Boy unfurled his fronds like a beautiful golden net, forming a basket that settled softly around the cretzina, cradling it, then pulling it close to him. The rumble of its complaining voice resonated against his carapace.

Boy giggled and rocked the little thing to and fro in the hammock of his many arms.

"What shall we name it, Mama?"

"Oh, no, my dear. We never name the merchandise."

"Oh." He peered through the long guard hairs that protected his hidden eyes.

"It is a cretzina, so you may call it that. But it's not a name, dear Boy."

"All right." He snuggled the little thing as it twisted and turned, looking to leap again.

She remembered that feeling herself, the attachment that had formed when she bestowed a name upon the fragile, beautiful keltizerian they'd smuggled under the very nose (speaking metaphorically) of a planetary imports director. At the conclusion of that long-ago deal, when the client gathered up his prize and strode off, the separation wrenched at her as harshly as after that last, parting argument with her parents, the one that cut her ties to Darrougha forever.

Though one might have expected separation from an animal to be easier, attachment has its own rules and knows no mercy. All the linkages in all her fronds burned as if struck by ionizing radiation. The step-by-step fraying of the detachment ripped at her mind, moment by moment, until the buyer boarded his transport and accelerated beyond that world's distant horizon. Her partner, the one who would be Boy's father, held her until the pain eased, then told her the secret.

Never name the merchandise.

Now, everything was changed. *He* had changed and severed more than his attachment to her, to their child. He'd broken the bond with their endeavor. All for another, for another's child, for another's ventures. It had just about driven him mad, she knew, that time with bonds in two directions tearing at him. By the time he'd changed, she'd lain in their nest each night pleading for his body to decide, whether it would cut him free to follow the other or keep him at her side.

• • •

Boy kept quiet, watching his parent with half his eyes and the cretzina with the rest. Mother seemed sad. Talking about names made her sad. Perhaps she was thinking ahead to the time, not so far off now, when he would be grown, and have his own name, and become his own self, with adult attachments.

Once she'd tucked the little cretzina into its pen, Mother eased herself out of her own skinsuit, and finally stretched her own fronds to embrace Boy. He bore the snuggle nearly as long as the cretzina had endured his own.

She settled him back down to his feet and whispered, "Iced cream?"

"Yes!"

There followed a blissful time, the cold confection on his tongues, the mess, the laughter and sweetness as they licked one another's fronds clean.

The cretzina watched them, maybe wakened by the noise.

"Well, Boy, do you want to feed it?"

Mother scuttled to the other case and pulled out an insulated packet. When she unsealed it, the savory odor of the cretzina's food morsels tickled Boy's olfactory membranes.

"Now, then, one piece at a time, no more than five altogether. If it doesn't seem eager, leave it be, all right?"

The cretzina satisfied itself with four of the crunchy little spheres, but Boy tucked one extra through the webbing of the containment, "For later," he said.

The bed was not good for comfort, being designed for a large bony frame, but Mother worked hard to make a nest for the night, using pillows and blankets. Boy decided he would rather sleep on the floor, close to the merchandise, so he could watch it until he fell asleep. Mother brought a blanket and a cushion and let him build his own nest.

Boy noticed something strange as he twirled into his place. It wasn't that his balance was wrong, but he spun differently; his mass had shifted.

"Mama?" he whispered.

"Yes?"

"I think I'm changing." He couldn't help sounding worried. His voicebox had compressed, adding a burr to his tone.

"Everyone changes, my dear. Don't let it worry you." Her voice flowed around him, warm and full of comfort. "You'll be just fine. I'm here."

"But, Mama?"

The lights in the room had begun to dim, and the walls seemed to recede, like a ship fading in the distance.

"Yes?"

"Will I run away? Like him? Will I leave you behind?"

One of her fronds flowed down from the bed and brushed his face, reminding him of the glow of attachment that bound them together.

"No, no, my dear. You cannot know, but he had reformed his attachments already. He meant to do well by us, truly he did, but his hearts were already elsewhere when the change came upon him. He couldn't help himself, darling Boy."

Boy couldn't forget, though. He'd known the moment was coming, that he'd be abandoned. Holding on hadn't worked, not at all. What if he hadn't tried so hard? He kept reaching for the sensation he knew he should remember — the glowing attachment to a living person, like the one that tied him to Mother. But he couldn't even feel the memory of it. When he retrieved his memories of the one he'd lost, they were cold, still frames of encounters with a kindly stranger. Boy felt strange, too. He always used to be scolded for his mischievous ways, but nowadays all he did was study, listen to Mama, and sleep.

Today, at last, a trace of the way he'd used to be had flowed back. All the sights and sounds — and flavors! — of the Truck Stop had opened up his mind. He could imagine having fun again. Mother had said, as soon as they delivered the merchandise, they would be free to seek out new lives. Soon, soon, everything would be all right.

Propped against the cushion, Boy peered into the shadows of the creature containment. Within, a row of glittery ovals peered back at him, four in all, though he knew the cretzina, like himself, had a total of five eyes on moveable stalks, as well as the two that stayed fixed in place, marking its front.

"Hello," he whispered. "Don't worry. Mama has found you a good place to go to."

The eyes blinked, one after another, making a moving line in the dark. A long feathery frond snaked through the netting and he held out one of his own. The cretzina's little animal fingers wrapped around his endmost tendrils, the ones most sensitive to touch and warmth, and tugged at him. Boy relaxed just enough to let the cretzina draw his finger-tendril up to the wall of the cage, where it could brush its mouthparts over his skin, tasting the essence of him. He held still, taking care not to pull back and injure the little thing's grasper. A name floated through his mind, a pretty name for a lovely creature.

"Ashoka," he whispered. "You are Ashoka."

The cretzina loosed his finger and stretched her frond out to brush Boy's face. Her featherings were down-soft, like his mother's touch, and he let Ashoka run her fingers over his eye-brow hairs and feel her way across each of his mouths. He kept the biting jaw tight-clamped, as before, and reveled at her fearless exploration of it.

With soft breaths whispering from the bed above, and Ashoka twirling in place, bouncing a little in the soft false gravity, Boy drifted to sleep happy.

4

GIRL

G IRL WOKE, jumping from memory to memory of the day past, and her eyes fell immediately upon Ashoka. The fuzzy white cretzina had learned she could scale the sides of her containment and hang from the top.

"Hello, Ashoka," Girl said, and she pressed one of her fronds to the side of the cage closest to Ashoka.

Girl felt strange. Everything about the day had shifted akilter, even the shape of her own self seemed odd. Not wrong, but ... different. The touch of Ashoka's feelers on her fronds filled her with comfort, but also triggered an anxiety she could not put a name to.

"Mama?"

"Yes, Boy?"

Oh.

"It's Girl, now, Mama."

The bedclothes rustled, and Mother's fronds unfurled to brush across Girl's face. That feather-light touch felt strangely cool, distant and unfamiliar. Girl tucked a frond through the cage netting, and Ashoka wrapped tight tendrils around her fingertips.

That's better.

"Well, now, my dear. That's all right. None of us can choose our time now, can we?"

"I don't know, Mama."

Nothing felt right. Girl curled up tight and hunkered close to the containment. Ashoka twirled a frond through the webbing and wrapped it around one of Girl's legs. It tickled, and a memory of laughter bubbled up inside her.

Mother said, "Our meeting with the client is soon, and then we will have the rest of the day to sort things out. You're all right, Girl, don't worry."

Girl didn't feel all right, but she knew how important this meeting would be, so she kept quiet. Mother scuttled around, tidying up the room, then came to her with a packet of food for Ashoka.

"I need to squeeze into my skinsuit. Would you like to feed the cretzina? If it's happy and well-fed, it will stay calm while we go to the meeting."

"All right."

Taking off a skinsuit went quickly. Not so clambering into one, and Mother was fussy about having it just so.

There would be plenty of time to feed Ashoka and play with her, before it was Girl's turn to get dressed.

Except Ashoka didn't like the food. She nibbled through half a morsel, then shoved it off to the side and rubbed her fronds at her mouth, brushing away remnants. Girl picked up the rejected food and sniffed it. Ashoka was right. It smelled ... wrong. Girl went to the case and found the left-over food from last night. Ashoka liked that. She ate it all up, skittered happily around her cage for a bit, then curled up and went back to sleep.

By then, Girl needed to get into her own skinsuit — with Mother's help, of course. It wasn't fair that the skinsuit couldn't change from being a boy, but she would have to make do. Girl always had trouble sorting out which fronds went to which arms and wriggling her fingers into place. Her legs had grown too long to fit the control frames for the skinsuit legs perfectly, so it took her several minutes to re-adapt to balancing on those two legs. The light gravity in the habitation ring helped a great deal, though, and soon enough she was hopping around the room, first on one huge flat foot and then on the other, with Mother laughing at her antics. That was always special, those times she could make Mother laugh. Girl clowned around until Mother smacked her pretty brown hands together and said, "It's time!"

Because, like Girl and Mother, the cretzina wasn't supposed to be found where humans lived, Mother had set up a trick to transport the little creature safely. She told Girl not to worry, that she'd done this trick before. "Here, gather up all the towels and ... oh, yes, some of the bedding, please."

Puzzled, but curious, Girl made good use of the skinsuit's arms to collect everything.

Mother took the bundle of cloth and stuffed it into the bathing compartment, then sprinkled it all with an awful-smelling reddish-brown liquid. She heaped the mess where the hostel proprietor had told them to place laundry.

"I will explain," Mother said, "that our wonderful event has happened. Humans, you see, are untidy. They haven't learned how to make eggs. I know, they are very clever, but they haven't mastered their own breeding as yet."

At last, Mother gathered up sleepy little Ashoka, all her insides filled with deliciousness, and bundled her into a funny little skinsuit that was very nearly an android, because it had no controls for the cretzina to operate. The skinsuit's face had big round eyes and was all covered with pink, wrinkly skin. It made wet, blurpy noises from time to time that set Girl to giggling, and she tried to emulate it with her own skinsuit.

"Blurp! Blurrrrp!"

Mother laughed along with her. Before, she'd been complaining of the inconvenience of having androids at security, as otherwise, she could have used the Baby skinsuit in the first place. Now, she had made a great game of it, and Girl soaked up both the game and the wisdom of it. They would fool the humans — and their silly machines — to achieve their goals with no harm done to anyone.

Finally, though, it came time to go. Mother packed up the cretzina's supplies into the little pink case. She carried the Baby in its perfume-smelly bundling, and Girl got to pull the supply case. She liked the bag's soft, magnetized wheels that supported its weight, while also keeping it from floating up when she pulled it along too energetically. The wheels made a *snickety-snick* sound on the deck that reminded her of Ashoka chewing her food morsels.

Activating her map, Mother led the way to the elevators and then to the Grand Mall, past the gift shop and the iced-cream store, all the way to a restaurant with a dim-lit entrance, right at the very edge of Green Quadrant. Tall figures that must have been androids, but not the nice shopkeeper kind, stood guard at a massive hatchway. Why it needed guarded, Girl could not puzzle out. In all the languages she could read, the hatch was labeled SEALED — NO ADMITTANCE — ORANGE. Even "orange" didn't make sense.

"Mama? Why is it orange?"

Mother seemed distracted, interrupted in studying the entry plate at the front of the restaurant. "Orange? I don't know, dear. Perhaps it is an upsetting color? Or perhaps it is some official's proper name."

Mother's fingers danced over the entry plate, and the door in front of them swung inward, making not even a fraction of a smidgen of a sound. Girl tapped her deck shoes a little, just to make a bit of noise, then followed as Mother led the way inside. The pink case squidged along behind Girl, adding its own comforting voice.

A tall human man, not only tall, but as wide as two men squished together, bowed to Mother then led them through the hush of the restaurant proper. Girl recognized six different non-human species, all conferring in low tones with human persons, facing them across smooth tables covered with white cloths and decorated with sparkling glassware containing interesting drinks in many colors. Nobody seemed to be eating, which made Girl feel hungry all of a sudden.

Their guide let them into a separate room, at the back of the restaurant, one with just a single white-clothed table and two glasses on it.

"Pardon, little fellow" said the wide man, giving a big, android-like smile to Girl, "I will bring a third glass."

Girl wanted to protest, but it wouldn't be good to upset Mother in the middle of a Negotiation.

It's all right, she told herself. *I am Girl disguised as Boy disguised as Human, and Ashoka is disguised as Baby, but I know who Mother is, and she knows I am Girl.*

•　　　•　　　•

Deralka spoke briefly with the maître d', to ask him to be sure that Girl's drink would not contain any intoxicants, and to ask if he might replace what the client had ordered for her, as her host had not yet appeared. As the oversized human reached the doorway, he stopped and backed up.

The client had arrived. A stocky human female in an overtight violet jumpsuit, she had iridescent hair teased to form a glittering partial sphere around her head. Her skin glowed with artificial color in somewhat-muted tones that echoed her hair. Everything about this woman screamed of elite society, the class that pleased themselves above all else.

The maître d' bobbed a bow in her direction, murmured something about a dirty glass, and soundlessly left the room.

The client obeyed the rules of negotiation, if not those of good taste. She invited Deralka to sit first, and gave Girl a pleasant greeting, treating her as Deralka's colleague, which seemed to brighten Girl's mood.

As per protocols, two chairs had free view of the entry, neither party suffering the anxiety of a door at her back.

Deralka signaled Girl to take the chair facing away from the door. They all settled comfortably at the table, but no one said anything until a narrow, tight-faced waiter appeared with a fresh glass for Deralka and a small one for Girl. She was proud to see her child — and business partner — sit quietly alert, sipping her sweet drink and offering a polite thank-you to the client.

The woman opened with, "So very glad you could make it." She barely touched her alcohol-tainted beverage, her eyes fixed on the blurping bundle at Deralka's shoulder.

Deralka provided the proper reply, "So sorry we were delayed. I hope you were not inconvenienced."

"No, no, I have made good use of the time."

Deralka's device having obtained sufficient data, she activated its spy feeders, providing the few illicit monitors in the room a tidy stream of suitably banal audio and video input. She sipped her drink and watched for her device to signal a satisfactory recheck. "Indeed," she said, then completed the signal phrase, "time is of the essence."

With the coded exchange completed, the client's demeanor shifted, her eagerness pressing to the fore. "Is that it?" she asked. "Can I see it?"

"Of course," Deralka said.

She carried the bundled-up Baby suit to the client and settled it on her lap, much as if it were in fact an infant human. The client's eyes twinkled and she giggled as she put one arm around its torso. The woman ran her hands along the sides of the suit, searching for releases.

Deralka relaxed just a smidgen. She'd worried that the client might find unpacking disturbing. "Allow me, it's a custom design. If you would steady the base, please."

"By all means."

With the client keeping the lower portion of the Baby suit balanced, Deralka could slip-release the tabs and glide the hidden seams open, folding away the noisemaking unit at the top, with those cute little flippy arms and their stubby fingers.

Within, the cretzina dozed contentedly, still digesting her sedative-laced breakfast. Aside from the practicality of having it calm during the transaction, that step ensured that it would be satisfied for a day or so, in the event her client experienced transit issues and could not unpack it for some time.

The client gazed at the little treasure and gave a pleased, admiring, "Ahhhh." She lifted one hand, paused, and said, "May I touch it?"

"Very softly, just the feathers if you would."

Deralka understood how deeply the desire to touch things resided in the human psyche. This critical moment would seal the transaction. Still, there was always the risk of an incautious client.

This woman, she could tell, was already well-sold, and that little frisson of delight would complete her decision-making. With utmost care, she glided a single fingertip over the crest of silver-white feathers that rippled above the cretzina's back, lifted by the light gravity and swaying with the air moving invisibly through the room. One of the cretzina's eyes rose on its stalk and turned slowly to and fro, then curled itself back down again.

"Marvelous," the human breathed.

Soon, very soon, Deralka and her child would complete their final transaction.

5

ASHOKA

A SERIES OF DULL NOISES caught Deralka's attention from the front of the restaurant. Probably nothing, but best to be safe.

"Is all to your satisfaction, then?" she asked, placing a warm smile on her own face while her audio sensors carried the sounds of distant voices.

"Very much so," the client said, keeping her voice low.

That pleased Deralka, to see merchandise go to such a considerate purchaser. Time to apply that final tiny nudge.

"For safety's sake, then, let's tuck her back in again, shall we? I'll walk you through the steps this time."

"Her?" said the client.

"Yes," Girl chimed in. "Ashoka's a girl cretzina."

"Ashoka." The client smiled at Girl. "That is a lovely name. Is it all right if I keep it for her?"

Girl nodded her head expertly, while Deralka's own fronds twitched within the safety of her skinsuit.

She named it. When did she name it? How long has it been?

As she worked through the simple, but critical steps of resealing the skinsuit and answering the client's questions, Deralka listened to approaching thumps and crackling sounds from beyond their closed door. The client either ignored the sounds or could not yet detect them. Before Deralka could even ask about concluding the transaction, the woman had sent the transfer, and both of their devices pinged, a half-octave apart, making a lovely little tune.

Her pleasure in the music — and what it meant for Girl and herself — was cut short as the door snapped open, swinging to clash against a cart set nearby. A tea-tray, set with little plates of cakes and other treats, lifted off the cart and sailed high, tumbling, until it smashed against the side wall. Shattered bits of crockery and ruined cakes fell to the decking. A pair of uniformed security officers stepped into the room and took up positions on both sides of the doorway. The one on the tea-tray side had to crunch over broken glass and sugary mush. After the briefest of pauses, the secretive law-man who had been tailing Deralka since yesterday strode through the door. Today, he had shed some of his secrets in favor of displaying a badge on his chest to identify him as Director of Security.

Deralka wondered if she should be able to read that notation from across the room, and decided, on balance, that she probably should not.

"Who are you?" she exclaimed, raising the pitch of her voice to indicate extreme alarm. She stepped between the enforcers and Girl, crossing her arms in a pose of defiance she'd seen in a drama, once.

"Code Enforcement," the law-man said. "What's all this, then?" His eyes went to the points in the room that housed those spy devices.

As if we'd tell you.

"You are out of order!" the client called out, still burdened with the Baby on her lap. It burbled and its arms jerked as if it was startled. "This is a perfectly legal engagement. I want your badge!"

The law-man gave the client a hard look, with narrowed eyes and down-curving lips. He unclipped his official badge and tossed it to the client — a perfect throw taking into account gravity, distance, air flow, and spin forces. The metallic sigil thumped onto the table within a few finger-breadths of the woman's hand.

She picked it up and had her device read its data. Then she frowned and tossed the badge in her hand twice. "You should be more careful. Had you missed, you might have struck Ashoka." She snuggled the Baby suit and kissed the top of its senseless head.

"You haven't answered my question," he said.

"What question?" Deralka asked.

"Yes," said Girl, standing up and peering around from behind Deralka. "What's the matter? Didn't you like the iced cream?"

"What?" It was his turn to be caught out.

"You went all the places, too, yesterday," Girl observed. "Did you get iced cream to take home, too?"

"That's enough!" the law-man said. "This is not about ice cream."

"Why not?" Girl said, her human eyes held wide and innocent.

He looked to Deralka. "We have it on good authority that a smuggling operation is taking place here. And I have verification that a massive funds transfer just took place at this node. You will not deny it."

Deralka hesitated, sorting through possible responses.

She need not have.

The client dove into the fray. "Indeed there has been and worth every little penny of it," she announced. Rising to her feet, the burbling Baby suit cradled in her arms, she continued, "This is a perfectly legal and above-board transfer of custody." Her device flashed, and the law-man's pinged, as a massive data file hurtled from her records to his.

Simultaneously, Deralka's own device pinged. She accessed the content, skimming more rapidly than any human might have done, while keeping her human eyes focused on the law-man as he processed the client's sending.

"Transfer of Custody Agreement," he read out. He looked from Deralka, with her skinsuit's smooth, flat anterior surface, to Girl, to the client, and then settled his eyes on the Baby. "You're selling a baby."

This time, Deralka was ready, her hearts reaching out in fellowship to this, her favorite client of all time. When had any client ever turned up so well-prepared? "No, it is a conclusion to a surrogacy arrangement."

"A what?"

The client took up the story. "This good lady has carried for me, all these long months, the child that my dearly-departed partner and I had so longed for all these many years. She has delivered to me my glorious Ashoka, healing me of my grief and pain. It is worth any price to me, and I am well able to afford the trifling amount that a peon such as yourself may consider to be massive. To me, it is merely just and proper payment for services rendered." She extended one puffy pastel-painted arm towards the doorway. "Get out, before you upset my baby!"

"Ah, um," said the law-man.

His companions exchanged glances behind his back. The one on the tea-tray side scraped goo off one shoe with the other shoe.

"Yes," said Girl. "Go away!"

The client eased herself back down to her chair, while the Baby suit energetically flapped its arms and gurgled like a dysfunctional waste disposer.

The law-man's eyes followed the client's every move. "What's that?" he said.

"It's a Baby, silly," said Girl.

"No, that." He moved into the room, his eyes riveted on the Baby.

He dared to point, despite the admonition in all the Truck Stop Guides against pointing one's indicator limbs in the direction of another living being.

"That," he said. "What's that?"

A wisp of a feathery tendril swayed from the edge of the skinsuit.

"It's nothing," Deralka said. "A feather fell from her hair. Don't be offending my client. Did you not hear her? She's an Elite."

Girl jumped down from her chair, directly in front of the law-man. "You're rude," she said. "You are not supposed to point things at people."

He grunted and let a little trace of a smile appear on his lips. "Sometimes, a grown-up must break rules in order to enforce the law, little boy."

"Girl!"

He rubbed a hand across his face, hiding a wider smile. The cretzina's tendril slithered out of sight. Deralka breathed a hidden sigh of relief.

"There, you see," said the client, sweeping her hand as if brushing away the feather. "It was nothing."

The law-man gave her a polite salute.

Then the entire seam down the side of the skin suit opened, the cretzina's frond-tip driving from top to bottom. A glory of white fronds thrust themselves through the open seam and curled back to grasp the edges. With a whining buzz, the cretzina pulled its body free, and its little rainbow-feathered legs kicked their brilliant colors under the lights.

The merchandise somersaulted to the floor, the little grasping feet making four distinct impacts on the deck — *click-clack-clack-click*. All five eyestalks extended, each at a different elevation and angle.

"Ashoka!" cried Girl.

Like a furry little gift box adorned with feathery streamers, the cretzina spun in place once, then hurtled towards the open door before any of the humans or either of the Darroughons could make a move. The creature vanished into the dimness of the restaurant proper.

Ignoring the possibility that anyone might realize her skinsuit was moving at a speed not normally attributed to humans, Deralka flung herself after the cretzina, with Girl clinking behind on her rented metal shoes.

The client shouted after them. "I'll be wanting a refund!"

•　　•　　•

Girl raced after Mother, terror clamped tight around her hearts.

Behind her, that rude man, the law-man who thought he was allowed to break rules, shouted, "Close the door! Door! Shut! Now!"

Ahead, Girl saw a dim blue rectangle — the inner door of the restaurant, where an incoming customer stood holding the door grip in one hand while maneuvering a lumpy black case through the opening. All her fronds splayed for balance, Ashoka leaped through the gap above the case. For a moment, she was a whirling ball of feathers catapulting into the outer passageway, then the customer's bag rolled free and the door thumped closed. Beyond, yet another customer opened the outer door.

"Ashoka!" Girl squealed.

The big man caught hold of Mother, but Girl kept running. Behind her, a loud crash was followed by bad words from the law-man. She grabbed at the door grip and hauled on it with all the power her skinsuit could produce. The inner door swung wide, gliding on its elegant hinges, and she jumped through the opening. The man with the bulky suitcase turned around, curious, and his bag fell over, blocking the inner door. Girl dodged the next incoming customer and *their* awkward luggage before the outer door could swing closed, and she dashed into the street.

Where was Ashoka?

There.

Scrabbling up the surface of the NO ENTRY PERMITTED hatchway, Ashoka moved from one handhold to another, quickly bringing herself well out of reach. The androids guarding the giant hatch stared stoically forward.

Girl ran to them and cried, "Help, help, my Ashoka is up there!"

"Retrieval squad notified," said the first android.

"Entry to Orange impossible," the other said. It made that fake android smile. "Do not worry. It is perfectly safe here."

Above them, Ashoka spread her fronds over a section of metallic gridwork just above the sealed hatch. A cretzina has perfectly drill-sharp retractable talons. Much like a Darroughon's. Not too surprising, given that both come from the same proscribed system. The androids, however, were not likely to know that, given they did not know that Ashoka was a cretzina.

Also, they did not know that Girl was a Darroughon.

A Retrieval Squad did not sound nice. They would not be nice to Ashoka.

Only Girl could save Ashoka now.

She reached for her skinsuit seals. The androids did not react as she slit open all the seams, tipped off her fake head, dragged her aching fronds out of those tubular arm-things, and disengaged her feet from the leg operators. Girl did not panic. Ashoka hadn't finished cutting off the grid yet. She followed all the steps Mother had taught her, to close the seals and leave the suit staring at the androids like a confused tourist.

She leapt for the first handhold on the hatch, her longest fronds swinging overhead to generate spin and her strongest ones springing on the deck like catapults to increase her range. As she flew, cartwheeling over the head of the taller android, she extended a pair of eyes and saw Mother and the mean man fighting to see who would get out of the restaurant first.

Moments later, Girl reached the top of the giant hatch. Below her, the vent covering clinked on the decking; above, the last of Ashoka's fronds rustled through the vent.
Girl followed.

6

PURSUIT

As SHE SQUEEZED into the vent opening, a strange sensation quivered through Girl's fronds and made her insides clench. The cold metal pressed closely around her, as if a monster had taken her into its jaws. She fought that fear, pushing all her fronds ahead of her and using her short little legs to press against the sides of the channel, pushing herself forward.

I should have gone feet-first, like Ashoka did.

Moments later, though, her fronds splayed out into a wide-open space, and she tumbled after them, sucking air in through all her spiracles. She'd landed in a wide square-edged metal tunnel. It stretched away in both directions, following the curve of the main ring's outer hull. Everything in this ring, she'd noticed, followed that curve one way or another. All she knew for certain was that she hadn't climbed up high enough to be anywhere near the hull itself. That made her feel safer.

The light from the narrower passage, behind her, spread a cone of brightness where she stood. In one direction, she could see the glow from another vent opening. In the other, she heard the *clickety-clack* of Ashoka's feet. Girl turned away from the light and opened her infrared eyes. Ashoka's heat signature blinked out abruptly. She'd either turned aside into another tunnel or disappeared along the curve of the ductwork.

Girl hurried after her.

Before, all those times she thought about attachment, Girl had envisioned silvery bands twirling from one to another, bands that made two people one being, their goals bound together. She saw their family as a triangle of silver light, infinitely connected forever and ever. Then Papa had vanished, into the skip-stream, severing their connection. No matter how hard she tried, Girl could no longer call up her father's name, guess where he might be, could not even imagine a journey to ask him — no, no, it was her, now — why, why she had gone.

Now, scuttling down a ventilation corridor in the dark, Girl saw the gleaming twirl of her attachment to Ashoka growing stronger and brighter the closer she came. It led her unerringly to the side-vent that Ashoka had taken, an inky-black channel no larger than the one they'd entered by. Girl held fast to that attachment, focused all her attention there, and forgot what Mother had told her so often: that a child must stay close, that only adults form strong attachments. She hadn't really believed it anyway, and that disbelief had let her hold on to her father's connection for a long, long distance.

Unhesitating, no longer even noticing the fraying strand reeling out behind her, Girl plunged into the darkness, all her attention on the creature she'd named. When the strand broke, she felt just the slightest tug of *what have I forgotten?*

The sound of Ashoka at work rattled against her ears. Soon enough, the glow of the cretzina's body heat showed against the cold, dark metal.

"It's just me, Ashoka," Girl whispered as she stretched her fronds cautiously forwards.

From the sound, the little creature had all her talons deployed. Ashoka was small enough to flip around in this channel, but Girl was constrained to one configuration. The cretzina made that low buzzing noise that Girl recalled from her objecting to being held, just last night. Girl kept her frond-tips out of range of Ashoka's feet, allowing a bit extra, as she didn't know how long those foot-talons might be.

She eased herself closer, until her infrared vision could overlap enough with the near-infrared to show where the metal had warmed at Ashoka's workings. With the added glow from her own body, perhaps Girl could make out details. She unfurled two of her own eyes, keeping the rest closed, just in case, and, indeed, she could now see they had reached a sealed vent-cover. She remembered the forbidding message on that giant hatch, so it made sense that the vent would not feed into that no-entry zone. Maybe the air in there was poisonous. Maybe it contained something dangerous in itself. Surely there were reasons. Grownups and humans weren't only annoying; often they knew important things.

How to persuade Ashoka of that, though? Animals don't know about danger in the world. Animals don't worry about what's coming next. They pay attention to what's happening now.

She thought back to their time in the hostel, and pushed herself backwards just a little, then sent forward a single frond, the same one that Ashoka had clung to last night. She wriggled the end-tips a little, to catch her attention.

Patience, Girl, patience.

The voice she made in her head sounded familiar, like someone she was supposed to remember.

Finally, Ashoka's mouthparts tickled the far tip of her frond, tasting the edges of her featherings. She wanted so much to scurry right up, but waited instead. Soon, she was rewarded by the touch of Ashoka's frond wrapping tight around hers, tightly enough that her fingers ached a little bit, but it was worth it.

Bit by bit, Girl scooted forward, without tugging on that physical bond. One by one, she let her own fronds glide forward, so that they would lie nearby, but not touching the cretzina.

Meanwhile, Ashoka drilled away at whatever there was at the end of the passage. It had to be something extraordinarily sturdy, if that neighboring sector was really so importantly cut off from the rest. So Girl didn't worry about that. She could let the drilling keep Ashoka distracted until her own fronds could snap in and enfold her. Someone would be proud of Girl, someone important to her, someone she couldn't quite put a name to just now, but it would come to her. Right now, she needed to focus on saving Ashoka.

Her last frond was gliding into place when everything went quiet. All she could hear was a faint hissing sound, one that at first she took for the sound of her frond sliding on the metal. But when she stopped moving, the sound continued. She scooted forward a bit, extending the rest of her eyes, searching the fuzzy glow of Ashoka and the surfaces her body heat lit up in the near-infrared, but there was nothing to see.

Slam!

A horrendous huge sound rang out behind Girl even as she was trying to investigate a small sound in front of her. The air swirled as if something had entered the passage behind her — or tried to enter and smashed hard into the narrow entry. She hoped that. She hoped that very much. There was no escape ahead of her. Poor little Ashoka clung tight, now with two of her fierce little tendrils.

If only she could turn around!

Whatever was back there, at least it couldn't get to Ashoka.

Girl kicked off the talon shields on her toes and flexed her legs, ready to fight whatever came.

A rapid series of thunking sounds rattled around the perimeter of the opening. Girl imagined a many-legged robot, armed with lasers, clunking its way towards her.

Her hearts rattled so fast, she could hardly tell them apart. She scrunched to one side to make a gap and squeezed one long frond backwards.

She expected any second to feel her fingertips being sheared away. What would it feel like? Would she just die of the pain?

Rumbling a little in her voicebox, without meaning to, Girl pressed that lonely frond further. It found a hard, flat surface rising vertically from the passage floor.

She scooted backward, balancing her sense of Ashoka's fingers ahead and her own frond-end exploring that mysterious new surface.

She ran her fingertips all over the flat thing, from floor to ceiling, from side to side.

They were closed in.

Alone.

Trapped.

Ashoka made her happy chirring sound, and Girl scooted back down the passage to be close to her.

"Well, Ashoka, looks like we have to drill our way out," she said. Girl pressed her own fronds across the panel in front, with the tiny hole where the hiss had come from now silent. "We're not dead. So I guess that means the air over there isn't poison."

The panel they faced had a half-dozen fixture points around its edges — probably the inward-facing ends of fittings that held the panel in place. Quivering a little with the sheer daringness of it, Girl unsheathed the talons on her two largest fronds and set to work on the fixture points furthest from Ashoka's workings.

Ashoka churred approvingly, and the grinding burr of the cretzina's drilling vibrated through Girl's body.

Girl sliced through the first fitting easily, but then she noticed the cretzina's noises had changed. She strained her infrared eyes to see, and realized that Ashoka had copied her. The little cretzina had begun to work on the panel's weak points, too.

"Good girl, Ashoka, good girl."

The cretzina rumbled happily as she worked.

7

ATTACHMENT

DERALKA'S ATTACHMENT with her child snapped almost immediately after Girl vanished into the vent. Desperately reaching for the broken connection, she swayed on her expensive human feet. This was worse than the departure of her mate, an event she'd been prepared for. Her joints burned with longing, like that time she'd thrown her attachment to a charming little creature, tied herself to it by the name that fell into her mind, only to lose connection in the inevitable transaction. Her fronds ached to stretch their full extent, grasp the lost girl, and bring her home, as her people had done in the forests of Darrougha since the dawn of time.

With the mis-named merchandise, her mate had helped her through the moment of disorientation. Now, she had no one to support her, no one to hold her until the shock would fade. No one else stood ready to cope with the client and the law and the androids who watched her child scramble up a wall and disappear into it.

"What in the seven blazing pits of Chrelchchth was that?" the law-man swore.

Deralka thought she might collapse. Thankfully, the skinsuit had sufficient autonomous functioning. That allowed her to remain vertical while her nerves sizzled and her stomachs argued as to which would be more fitting: emptying or filling. The smell of active flesh so close by triggered atavistic impulses, but her sensory inputs were moderated by the skinsuit's processing systems, enough so that she did not even make a twitching motion in the direction of the startled security officer. She had the taste of him, though, swirling over her olfactory membranes. Her image of the world — this narrow, confined world of recycled air and plasteel — swayed.

"What the *hell* was that?" he demanded.

His hand wrapped around her skinsuit's wrist, which the software translated to the sense of an embrace, and the world steadied. His heat signature flowed from his core through his limbs, and into her skinsuit, transmitting a warmth that drew her out of that frozen state.

"My child!" she cried.

The moment of honesty went unnoticed, as he focused on the unmoving skinsuit standing in front of the guards, while Deralka gazed at the vent opening that had consumed Girl.

A gang of new androids came thumping towards them, spinward from the entry to the mall, sending tourists and merchants scattering inboard and outboard. The androids guarding the gate reacted first. One of them picked up Girl's abandoned skinsuit. The unoccupied body flopped like an unconscious person.

The other android slapped a hand-panel at the side of the giant hatch. For a moment, Deralka expected the hatch to swing open. The law-man, too, must have had the same notion, because he moved backward, drawing her with him while shouting to bystanders, "Stay back! Stay back!"

Instead, a narrow opening, no wider than a single android, and glowing with light, blinked into being at the side of the hatch. The android carrying Girl's suit vanished within. A third android, identical to the others, stepped out. The shining door vanished. Again, two androids stood before the gate.

The emergency crew arrived. The law-man stepped between them and the hatch.

"Calum Schoonover, Director of Security, Green Quadrant," he called out, and his device radiated data to all of the androids.

Deralka's device reached into the stream and retrieved data on the man. Unattached, but formerly so, a parent himself, financially insecure, decorated in battle, yet now eking out a living as the human face of an artificial police force. Deralka's emotions swirled, seeking attachment, drowned in pain.

"Calum," she said, but softly, not to interfere with his negotiation.

The androids had halted at Schoonover's order, but their sensory apparatus focused on the hatch at the boundary. Deralka observed suddenly that these androids differed from the guards, not in their overall structure, but in the designs on their torsos. The approaching squad bore sharply-defined swirls of green embedded in their plasteel surfaces, while the guards had tracings of orange.

One of the androids — it was difficult to tell which, they were so alike — announced, "Incursion to Orange Quadrant. Emergency action required. Stand aside."

Her device tapped the details as they flowed to Calum's device, but nothing in that mass of information could help her. More notably, no communications flowed from the Orange Quadrant androids. They stood like statues in front of the great hatch, just as when Deralka and Girl had arrived.

"Orange Quadrant has already taken action," Schoonover replied. "Obtain information on action taken."

Deralka knew that the emergency squad androids were communicating with each other, but they remained silent for a moment or two.

"Recommendation accepted," they said.

So the implications she'd gleaned from Schoonover's dataset were accurate. The Director of Security did not so much command the security forces as assist them and provide guidance. It would take a remarkable individual, Deralka concluded, to navigate the channel between command and service. Who knew what the android forces were originally designed for? Perhaps they were soldiers, and so required an interlocutor with the correct degree of command.

Two androids peeled off from the squad and approached the pair at the hatch. Modulated, secure data transfers ensued. Deralka fumed that her equipment could not capture more than a scattered sense of … conflict.

"They are not happy with each other, Director Schoonover," she observed.

His head turned, and he looked at her with one of those hard-to-decipher expressions. "Oh?"

"Do you see? The green androids are maintaining greater distance with the orange androids than they do with one another."

"Yes." His voice kept an even modulation, as if he were speaking to distract her. "Orange androids tend to be … argumentative. Their primary task is maintaining their perimeter."

She looked up at the dark rectangle where the cretzina and Girl had vanished. The two of them had traveled some distance in a tight space, before she had lost contact with Girl. "What is that up there?" She lifted her skinsuit's arm and pointed to the vent opening.

"Where the creature went? I'm not sure." He turned to the nearest green android. "Define the contents of the rectangular opening on the wall above the hatch."

The android aimed its sensor grid at that area of the wall. "Nothing." Its flat metallic voice made it sound less sentient than the entry-inspection android.

"What do you mean?" Calum's voice had a burr of frustration to it. He might have been a Darroughon himself.

"It is nothing. Emptiness. A channel with nothing in it."

"Nothing? Be specific. What fundamental elements are observed at that location?"

"Iron, chromium, nickel, oxygen, carbon, nitrogen."

"Is that all? Steel and air? All you'll tell me is that there is a channel there with air in it?"

"Air. Correct. Inside the plasteel, it is air."

"Why tell me it was nothing? Explain."

"When humans see air, they call it nothing. The Security Director is human. Therefore, it is nothing."

Schoonover's face bore an expression that Deralka recognized. He wanted to kill the sarcastic android. It was such a sweet thought. She wished she could do that for him. Her talons slid from their sheaths, just a little, an itch wanting to be scratched.

"You're telling me that *thing* went into an air vent?"

"Correct."

"Why is there an air vent connected to Orange Quadrant?"

"It is not."

"What? Repeat. Clarify."

"The air vents connect within Green. Orange is not connected."

Deralka's feathers ruffled within the skinsuit's arms.

It's a pressure-normalizing channel. It will connect elsewhere along the perimeter.

"Where are the other vent openings?" she asked.

The android did no more than turn its sensor grid towards her. Its face returned to pointing at Schoonover.

The law-man repeated Deralka's question.

"Equidistant along the sectional."

"How many are there?" Deralka could sense Calum's increasing annoyance at the level of information he was getting.

"Thirty-six."

She saw Calum's device flicker, calculating staffing and requirements. "Dispatch crews to each vent opening."

"Already in progress."

Calum's shoulders tightened. "Orders."

Deralka wondered if he meant he was ready to accept orders from the android crew or ...

"Provide orders," the android stated.

"Locate unidentified organism. Capture. Do not destroy. It is evidence. Understood?"

"Understood."

"Transmit order."

"Transmitted."

If security androids had expressions, Deralka would have expected this one to be showing disappointment. How many opportunities does a security guard get to kill something? Calum had just taken that option off the table.

"Thank you," she said.

He looked back at her, and a variety of interesting expressions ran over his face. He had no idea what she was thanking him for. How could he know she'd been listening to the android subchatter on this side, catching bits and pieces like *laser-equipped channel bot* and *fire on sight.*

He may well have just saved Girl's life.

"You're welcome, madame," Calum replied. "And now you are under arrest."

Before she could process what he'd said, he snapped restraints on both arms of her skinsuit and signaled two of his green-ornamented androids. Even through her skinsuit, his gaze had the intensity of command.

He's military, she thought. *Was he in a war? One of our wars?*

The androids stepped forward and caught her by the arms of her skinsuit.

"But ... Calum ... what about Girl?" she protested.

"The androids are negotiating on that matter. It's an Orange Quadrant issue. Out of my jurisdiction. Meanwhile, there is the matter of an illicit transaction, the release of an unpermitted organism, and, I suspect, more concerns will emerge."

"You can't do this!" She pushed her suit's eyes wider and eased the pitch on the voice up several notches. "I demand my rights!" She activated her device and spewed out appeals for legal assistance as noisily as any overprivileged tourist.

From unseen recipients somewhere in the Grand Mall, she began to receive offers, most entirely inappropriate to her situation, but all serving to muddle local communications.

Meanwhile, her sendings bounced through the station's network, the encrypted instruction set riding along, tunneling through the channels to its destination. Somewhere out on the docking rim, her ship would be readying itself for departure.

The four androids conferring at the gate had taken far too long in their discussion, for entities who communicated through data, not speech. Deralka had the sense more was going on behind the scenes.

Conflict, she thought. *These parties are in active conflict. What is it about Orange?*

The tourist guides had nothing to say other than "Keep Out."

What was the law-man waiting for? A movement at the restaurant entry caught her eye. The client was emerging; keeping her face turned away, she hurried down the mall. Almost immediately after that, the law-man's human associates emerged, one of them dangling the unoccupied Baby suit from one arm. Schoonover waved to them and began to walk back down the Mall. The androids flanking Deralka forced her to turn around and follow.

Her device began to register a series of tidy encrypted messages from the client. Probably she still hoped to somehow acquire her prize, but the likelihood had become vanishingly small. At best, the cretzina would be recovered by station security and shipped back to Darrougha under lock and key. At worst, the hazards to a transportation crew from the little charmer would be measured against its value, and it would be destroyed outright.

Girl, though, Girl might be saved.

8

ORANGE QUADRANT

L IGHT FLOODED into the narrow passageway as the vent cover finally fell free.

As her eyes adjusted, Girl realized the light was not so much a flood as a faint trickle. It was because the vent was so dark that the hall below seemed bright.

Compared with the huge, bustling Grand Mall, this place seemed to be in a different universe.

The mall felt almost like being outdoors — a vast space with structures lining the walkway, all at different heights, but each pointing at the station's hub, the perspective along the curve of the station making everything seem to loom overhead. This new space reminded Girl of the time they'd delivered merchandise on Almadestra, where all the high officials worked alone in little boxy rooms in rigid mazes built into tall towers lit by artificial light, even though their world was full of color and life ... beyond the walls. Here, the mysterious sector seemed to be nothing more than a bland hallway lined with closed doors and shadowy alcoves that might be branching-off corridors. The silent, empty corridor stretched out of sight around the station's curving hull.

Nothing moved but drifting specks of dust, jiggled around by the air they floated in. Her sides itched as she slid air filters over her spiracles, and she hoped Ashoka's instincts would drive her to do the same.

Girl stretched her fronds to feel the surface just outside their refuge. It was ordinary plasteel: cool to the touch, but smooth, not eaten away by acidic gases or fractured by weapons fire. Whatever the Orange sector's purpose, it wasn't to contain a poisonous atmosphere or conceal some ancient conflict.

Before Girl had even formed a notion of entering the place, Ashoka had already scuttled over the edge.

"Ashoka!" Girl cried, reaching for the cretzina with two fronds and scrabbling for handholds with two more.

They'd traveled some distance from the hatch, though, and here the wall had nothing to offer. Frantically, she reached back with all that she had left and drove her talons into the edges of the passageway, making her own limbs into a lifeline. Her reaching fronds brushed across the back of Ashoka's carapace, and she had just barely time to twirl her fingers around the cretzina's legs as she fell. They made for an odd sort of daisy-chain assemblage — the ragged-edged vent opening, Girl's long fronds, Girl herself, her reaching fronds, Ashoka, and Ashoka's fronds. The dust in the air swirled as Ashoka reached for the floor.

Girl extended her eyes as far as they would go.

Yes.

The smooth, dusty floor was now barely a finger-length below Ashoka's frond-tips. The little cretzina would easily manage that drop.

Girl's fronds ached, but more from the wrenching they'd taken in stopping the fall than from any strain in the moment. One by one, she uncurled her fingers from Ashoka's legs, keenly aware of those hidden foot-talons. Mother had put covers on them, but this had been quite a scramble, nothing like a quiet ride inside a skinsuit. With a *clink* and a rustling of fronds, Ashoka dropped to the floor below.

I can't drop now. I'll crush Ashoka.

Girl hung from her finger-talons and waited. Presently, Ashoka shifted to her feet, swirled her fronds up over her back, and began to scuttle on down the corridor. That had given Girl time to think of how to ease her own fall. She didn't relish the idea of chasing after the cretzina with her own fronds mangled in a drop onto that hard surface. She released one talon, and jammed it into the wall a short distance below the vent, then did the same with the other, a little further down. Step by step, she hammer-clawed her way down the wall, leaving a clear path that any pursuer might follow. Then again, she hadn't heard any pursuit. Besides, the vent passage was sealed tight on the other side, wasn't it?

With her much longer legs, she quickly caught up with Ashoka, who clicked along determinedly, probably searching for another hidey-hole to dive into. For the time being, Girl kept a sharp eye out for such dodge-holes, and kept pace with the anxious cretzina.

She spoke soothingly as they walked along together, in this strange, empty place. "It's all right, Ashoka. We'll find our way back. You'll see."

Orange Quadrant had too many warning signs on it to be a safe place. Her hearts rattled.

A steady beat of sound rumbled in the deck plates below her, a two-beat sound, the sound of footsteps.

Girl unfurled her fronds and tested her talons, ready for battle.

Ashoka hurried onward.

The corridor ran straight as an arrow from the wall they'd entered at towards, Girl guessed, the next quadrant in the ring. According to the map in her device — left behind with her skinsuit — this sector of the Truck Stop was

Unknown Territory. She'd imagined a garden of strange life-forms, with many-colored jungle plants having filled in all the nooks and crannies, and mysterious creatures peering out from their hideaways.

A wonderful, dangerous, beautiful place.

It would not be a long, dusty corridor, not even one with an unseen opponent walking towards them, somewhere around the curve of the deck. At the very least, the predator would approach by leaps and bounds and pounce upon them before they could become aware of its presence.

Instead, the footsteps slumped along, one by one.

At last, the feet showed themselves: shiny gold-colored shoes in the right shape for human feet. Step by step, the legs came into view — thinner than the average human's, and oddly long, those were the same warm yellow-brown color as the feet. Their skin — or was it clothing? — seemed smooth and shiny, almost metallic, but not quite.

Is it an android?

Something about the way it moved seemed more natural than mechanical, but this station had some very complicated androids, like the one she'd met in the gift shop.

It took a long time for there to be more to see than legs. If that was a human, it was a very tall one.

Finally, a torso began to come into sight, like it was oozing through the ceiling. Girl knew it was an illusion, an effect of the ring's curvature, but it was more fun to imagine something weird emanating from the outside of the station, perhaps a mysterious traveler from the black hole itself.

Girl kept pace with Ashoka, wondering in each moment if she should grab the cantankerous animal and run the other way. But where could she go? Back into the vent? And then what?

At last, a head appeared, a smooth ovoid with a human-like face, but without the dangling or puffed-out hair that humans liked to decorate their heads with. Now that she could see the whole, she was convinced that it was neither a human nor an android, but some kind of humanoid she'd never seen before. Rather than the interesting complexities of humans or the balanced symmetries of androids, its body shape formed a pair of compressed, truncated cones, their dull ends pressed together, giving it a narrow waist. Its legs stretched long, to match long arms, making it out of scale with itself. Even more odd, the whole shape of this being seemed to ripple under the poor lighting and the hovering dust, so that each moment it looked different than in the moment before.

Girl had no disguise here. This would be her first unshielded encounter with a humanoid.

She knew — and hoped it did not know — that her opponent advanced towards, not a helpless child and a cute pet, but a healthy young Darroughon and a full-grown cretzina. What would be the best way to defeat it? Cut the muscles that made its legs work, so that it couldn't run away? Slice off its fingers so it couldn't summon help with its device? Better yet, cut away the device itself, first, and set it aside, to use later. Girl rasped her biting teeth together, rousing herself up.

I've never ever had to fight anybody.

I can do it.

For Ashoka.

Suddenly, Ashoka skreeled to a halt, her feet driving score-marks into the floor. She skittered backwards a few steps, then twirled, her fronds sailing in a tight spiral, like a whirlwind, and dashed behind Girl.

Girl flexed her talons and curled a pair of fronds around the frightened creature.

"Don't worry, Ashoka, I'll save you," she rumbled, as softly as she could.

In response, a familiar tickling and scraping fluttered across her back, and then a weight pressed where her carapace dipped. Ashoka's fronds whispered across Girl's face as she curled up and hunkered down on top of Girl. The sense of power and responsibility frightened her.

If the humanoid has a Secret Weapon and defeats me, what will become of Ashoka?

She thought on the days she'd traveled with other Darroughons, with the family that now seemed so distant, no longer a part of her the way Ashoka was. Never had she seen either of them leap to attack, always they had feinted with words and dodged with schemes, and always they succeeded in their escapes.

So I will do the same. I won't attack unless I have to. I'm not as clever as those adults, but I'm cleverer than any non-Darroughon might think.

9

NOT IN THE GUIDEBOOK

GIRL HELD HER GROUND as the humanoid approached, at each step seeming more an ordinary physical being and less a wavering mirage. She curled her fronds over her back, knowing they wouldn't truly conceal little Ashoka. One by one, she drew her talons back into their sheaths. She hoped that wouldn't turn out to be a mistake, but, still, she could unsheathe them in the time it took for a frond to fly out to its full length.

Just in case.

The footsteps vibrated up through her toes, from the dull, metallic floor. For a moment, she missed the way her skinsuit muffled those sensations for her.

She'd been warned — but could not recall who told her — that humanoid-types found beings with more than two eyes upsetting and that eyes on stalks were considered nothing less than horrors. Girl tucked her eyestalks well down into her fluff, lifting her feathers a bit to help disguise them further.

To her relief, the humanoid seemed to have no weapons, though it could have crushed her underfoot — had Girl been the fragile innocent she made herself appear.

It stopped a safe distance away, almost exactly at the length of her longest fronds — including extended talons. Then it descended, bending one leg to rest on its knee, folding its funny bony arms so they rested on its leg.

"What have we here? Are you lost?" it said, using — she was unsurprised to hear — the shared language all the humans seemed able to use, though most relied on translation devices to manage the special words or whole languages unique to their homeworlds or spacefaring clans. Humans, according to her studies, formed attachments to groups, not so much to individuals.

"It's just me, Girl," she replied, working hard to make her voicebox buzz out the words well enough. When she heard what she'd said, a new sense of uncertainty stole over her. It reminded her of last night, when she was talking to Ashoka, and that sensation of change had ruffled over her.

I can't be changing again, can I? she wondered.

She wished there were someone nearby she could ask about that.

Never mind. No matter what, I'll protect Ashoka.

"Hello, Girl," said the human.

Girl kept both of her visible eyes on it as she listened. It hadn't introduced itself, so she didn't say hello back.

She wished she could use the rest of her eyes without being frightening. In her skinsuit, she could make full use of the skinsuit's input stream. There, she could swap to whichever of her real eyes could be of best use, sometimes more than one real eye taking in the same data stream.

"Who is your friend?"

"Ashoka is mine."

The human made no move to take Ashoka or to hurt either of them, so she did no more than rock her fronds to and fro a little, to keep them limber.

"Hello, Ashoka."

As she studied the humanoid's face, it dawned on Girl at last just what it was that confused her about it. She couldn't decide its gender. Humanoids generally made great efforts to be sure anyone looking at them could tell. This one wore plain clothing the same color as its skin, arranged to disguise any distinctive shapes underneath, instead of emphasizing the parts humans were most interested in. Its face had both smooth, rounded shapes and sharp, forbidding shapes, of the kind that humans called *feminine* and *masculine*. Once again, she wondered if it were really an android, but she had her infrared eye open, and it was a living being, not a machine, definitely. Maybe it wasn't a human, then. Maybe it was something else.

"Are you a boy or a girl?" she decided to ask.

Humans liked that sort of question from a child. It always made them laugh, and humans had difficulty doing hurtful things while laughing.

It didn't laugh. "I am myself," it said. "Just as you are yourself and Ashoka is Ashoka's self."

"Oh. What's your name, then?" Girl wasn't quite satisfied with the reply. She wondered if that was some kind of trick. It didn't seem like it was making fun of her. It seemed very serious.

"I am the caretaker."

"That doesn't sound like a name," Girl said. Her voice buzzed more harshly than she meant it to, but it hadn't answered her right, had it?

"Ah." It coughed, a gravelly, grindy sound. "One might say the same of yours, Girl."

Girl buzzed her dissatisfaction, even though doing that might be heard as rude.

The human made a grunting sort of laugh. "No one's used my name in such a long time. It's very difficult to say, even for me. Please. Just call me Caretaker. There is only one of me, so it is as good as a name, isn't it?"

"Who do you take care of?" She couldn't envision this being entertaining a pod of human children. Human children wanted to have fun all the time, not just when they were eating iced cream.

"I take care of the station." It made a slow, easy gesture, with just one arm, to indicate the whole of the Truck Stop — or at least this sector of it. Girl appreciated that it took care not to startle her. She wasn't completely sure she could control all of her defense responses.

"The whole station? You're not in the guidebook." She rattled her voicebox a little to show that she meant that as a challenge. It felt good to do something aggressive, even if it was just a vocal trick.

"Well, now, all these newcomers have their own ideas, and they are doing well enough, if I do say so myself. So, yes, Girl and Ashoka, I take care of the whole station, though I myself keep to this portion that they have left to me. I do believe I have made it clear that the sector is mine alone, to do with as I please."

"You haven't done much with it."

Girl lowered a frond and extended one finger to trace out a spiral shape in the dust on the floor. The particles floated up and swirled around prettily. She made another spiral, in the opposite direction, and the floating motes danced around each other.

"For now," said Caretaker, "it is enough to have my boundaries established. There's plenty of time, and I have my androids keeping watch, so I know how the rest of my station is faring."

"Your androids? Your station?"

Girl couldn't help it, another pair of eyes lifted up in her surprise. Hurriedly, she retracted them back into her fluff and waited for the humanoid to begin yelling or attacking her.

Instead, it wrinkled the skin above its eyes, almost as if mimicking her. "We can talk about my androids later. Tell me, have you perhaps lost something?"

"Me?"

"Yes. My androids have brought me a thing that looks as though it belongs to you."

"Really?"

She thought about iced cream. She thought about the yipping-animal toy back at the hostel. She thought about the fancy kit to build her own model of the station, that was in the big box at the hostel. None of those things were lost, though the iced cream was all gone. What could be missing?

Caretaker held out one of its hands. "Come with me. I'll show you."

Girl looked at the hand. She imagined what it would look like if she sliced at it, just a little. She thought she could fillet away all the meat on it in very little time. But it was a passing fancy. Girl might be hungry, but she wasn't that hungry.

She lifted a frond, but didn't place it in Caretaker's hand. That could be risky, for both of them.

"All right," Girl said. "Show me. If it isn't mine," she offered, "I might be able to help you figure out whose it is."

10

SECURITY

WITH TWO SECURITY ANDROIDS walking her skinsuit for her, Deralka withdrew a pair of fronds from the false arms and accessed the more-complex systems she maintained in the interior space. She studied the ongoing string of messages from her client. The honorable thing to do, and the practical action, in this moment, was to make a refund. That would maintain her reputation. She could try again, perhaps with this same client. That is, she and Girl could start over. She would retrieve Girl, and the cretzina, and they would make that final transaction a reality. Somehow.

The weight of their financial situation weighed heavily. If there were some way to keep the funds, to tide them over, that would be ideal. This client appeared willing to negotiate, but there were no guarantees, no way to assure her the cretzina would survive this misadventure. The contract was already null and void. They would have to start fresh.

She checked accounts, verified the client's preferred deposit location, and sent the funds back. If she could extricate the Baby suit from the law-man's clutches, it might possibly be returnable, for a prorated refund, but she couldn't manage to think that far ahead.

Her fronds trembled. *Girl. I must think of Girl.*

Residents and visitors alike stared at their cavalcade: Calum in his uniform, the officer in front of him carrying a seemingly-deceased human infant, and a tall human woman being escorted by cold-eyed security androids. Knowing humans, she felt sure the rumor spreading was that this woman had murdered a baby.

"Hey!" she cried out. "This isn't right! I haven't done anything! You're targeting me just because I'm a new arrival!"

Calum turned around and stopped. "Cut it out."

She made the skinsuit suck in a huge breath and triggered an operating mode she'd labeled *hysteria*. "The Orange androids stole my child!" she shrieked. "Won't anybody help me? He's framing me with a fake! Help! Help!"

Several people advanced towards their party. One of them tried to grab the Baby suit, but the android lifted it out of reach.

An Andolian stretched its long, hairy blue arm to poke a hand into the open skinsuit. "Hey!" she shouted to the crowd. "It's true! There's just plastic and metal and electronics in there!"

People pressed closer, and Calum stopped, held up his badge and drew his weapon. It looked to her like nothing more than a simple stunner, but it was enough to make them stop.

"Listen up!" he shouted. "No one is accusing this visitor of hurting a baby! This object is evidence in a crime of property, not a crime of violence. Everyone step back, or I'll see you all fined for obstruction! You are all being recorded. This will be your only warning!"

People grumbled, looked around for the invisible spybots, and stepped out of the way.

Somebody called out, "Good luck, lady! The Truck Stop is a safe haven!"

The Andolian, her wide, cobalt-blue eyes gleaming with curiosity, waited until Deralka was being hauled past and called out softly, "If you need legal funds, I'll buy that off you!"

Deralka gave her a warm smile, but shook her head. She'd do better with the skinsuit dealer, and, besides, there was Darroughon technology embedded in that thing.

Deralka couldn't stop second-guessing herself. She hadn't anticipated being *arrested*. Had she acted more quickly, she might have stripped off the skinsuit and torn her own way from this sector to the next. If Girl were trapped in the Orange Quadrant, what was the chance those enigmatic androids would bring her back? Then again, if the child was still skittering along in that ridiculous vent channel, what could Deralka accomplish other than revealing herself? To say there was no love lost between humans and Darroughons would be very much an understatement.

Through her work, Deralka had come to an uneasy respect for the creatures. Virtually all of the clients who'd engaged their agency had been humans, of one variant or another. They had such a fascination with the little creatures they sought out as pets — a hobby uncommon among other species. It gave her the feeling there might be more to humans, ultimately, than met the eye. It seemed to her that having enough empathy and affection for a creature to care for it properly spoke well for this often-problematic intelligent species. This species that had *captured* her.

They lead her directly to the security office, one managerial unit of many embedded in the official structures that flanked the elevator bay. Deralka's escort marched her straight through the doors, past a roomful of staring android faces, and into a boxed-in room with carefully-arranged images on one wall and sealed cabinets ranged across the others.

The Security Director's office, no doubt.

Yes.

Schoonover moved to take the traditional position: ensconced behind a broad desk made to look as though it was wooden. She could tell by looking at it that it was plasteel, but then again, she didn't use human eyes. He didn't look at her, but instead began shifting papers around on the desk. If there was an organization to those materials, it wasn't apparent to her.

"There." Schoonover ordered, and the man with the Baby suit dropped it on a table near the desk.

Could she possibly get away with explaining the purpose of her operation? She was making humans happy, after all. Her clients appreciated not only the beauty of the creatures she collected for them, but also the dangers they presented. Today's client would have given the cretzina a secure home and a long, pampered life. Deralka and her mate had invested a great deal to extract an animal that at home was treated as a pest.

She knew that traffic in exotic beasts lay outside the boundaries of most planetary systems' laws — the family specialty being the colorful, clever, and dangerous inhabitants of worlds such as her own, those proscribed by humans for one reason or another. But this was the Truck Stop, nobody's homeworld, and a facility founded on the leave-it-be principle espoused by founders that everyone knew to be more criminal than Deralka could ever be.

"Sit." Schoonover ordered.

The security androids led her in front of the desk and all but shoved her — or, rather, her skinsuit — into a chair.

How much could she safely reveal? That the client had not been purchasing a baby ... well, that story was over. That the animal he'd seen came from Darrougha? Probably not a good idea.

The cretzina was a product of the same glittering forests of crystal and iron her own people had evolved in. Her studies of the humans' water-world home had taught Deralka that their oceans were much like Darrougha's forests. All except the least of the lowest orders were predators, each more deadly than the last. On their emergence from Darrougha, the Darroughons had torn through their opponents just as they'd torn through their competitors. Fragile humans appeared to have survived by leaving their oceans early, but they had kept the instinct to fight to the death when in peril.

So, no, revealing herself could not be an option. How to explain the Baby suit and its contents? Could she represent herself as a clumsy human intermediary, a smuggler, but a hapless one, caught in the crosshairs of misfortune?

Calum stopped fidgeting with his papers and looked from her to the Baby suit and back again. "So, what's inside that thing? What are you?"

"I beg your pardon?" He'd already jumped to the correct conclusion? Or was he merely guessing? Or something else?

"This thing —" he left his desk and hefted the Baby suit. It waggled its arms and drooled, despite being unoccupied.

Nobody turned it off.

"The androids have declared this 'container' of yours to be proscribed technology."

"Proscribed?"

"Proscribed doesn't mean unknown. We know where this thing came from. How did you get it?"

"I paid for it. What do you imagine? It doesn't seem that strange to me. It's just a fancy container. It met my client's needs. Where does it come from, then?"

Yes. Throw the question back to the questioner.

Calum slapped his desk and papers fluttered even more out of order. "No games. Just answer my question. It's a simple one. Do I have to wait until the androids funnel the video back to me?"

"What question, Calum?" She made her face into a smile, but one she'd learned included an element of sadness. The menu options were extensive for cheerful expressions with contradictory undertones.

"What was in this ... robot baby?"

Deralka trained her eyes to one or another of the skinsuit inputs, to study the law-man's expression. Like many in his profession, he'd mastered basic control over his features. The temperature patterns beneath his skin betrayed underlying emotional responses. She looked over his shoulder, to the row of still images affixed to the wall. They displayed a sequence of a human man and woman together with a child, as the little one evolved from the size of the Baby suit to a creature not much more mature than Girl's skinsuit. A photo of the adults alone ended the sequence. Unlike the rest, in this image neither human bared their teeth. The breakages in her own family gave Deralka a thought she might make use of.

First, though, she activated a skinsuit function she'd used very little over the years. First one, then another, warm, salty droplet formed in one eye, overflowed the capsule's lubrication capacity, and flowed down her cheek. At the next inhalation, her skinsuit made a thick, wet sound.

"It seems you, too, have lost a child," she tested.

His eyes went wide, then narrow, and the flush under his skin rose up, deepening the color there from a crunchy, aged-propellant hue to one like a red-tinged jet-insulation material. As her options opened, her hearts began to beat a little easier.

His gaze went from her, to the Baby suit he'd left on the table, and back. She needed to decide quickly between drowning her opponent in truth or burying him in lies.

Ordinarily, she preferred a well-constructed set of lies, but in an urgent situation it could be difficult to keep track of their relationships and dependencies.

"To answer your question," she said, before he could speak again. "Yes, it is a container. My client required a certain type of delivery for the merchandise. One appropriate to her cover story. You understand."

He leaned back and tapped his fingers on the edge of the desk, a rolling motion that made a quick, four-beat pattern, like a pair of hearts pulsing in sequence.

Confession of a minor offense deters suspicion of the major offense.

"I will acknowledge it. The merchandise is not approved for import to her homeworld."

His mouth made a straight line. "What homeworld would that be?"

She shrugged. "It is not required in our contract for her to disclose that particular, simply to notify us if that is an issue. In this case, for example, we chose not to risk a merchandise transfer there. Less convenient, but more safe."

"Merchandise? The thing that ran out the door? What was it? How did it climb the wall? Why would it go into the ventilation system?"

Just how much had he seen? Both Girl and the cretzina? If so, why not say "things" and "were" and "they"? Human language had those two number conventions — singular and plural — and they used those rigorously.

Deralka interlocked the fingers of her skin-suit. The illusion of close connection between her real fingers gave her a little comfort. "I am not at liberty to say, at risk of violating my client's trust." If she could stretch this conversation, he might let slip whether he'd seen the animal as well as the child. From her perspective, the last of the cretzina's fronds had been barely visible when the adults exited the restaurant, but Girl had been right at the vent by then.

"Isn't your contract null and void now? Your client ditched you —" he rapped on the desk — "and demanded a refund —" another rap — "then left you holding the bag. As it were." He shot a glance at the Baby suit and returned to tapping his fingers. She tamped down her audio inputs. He wouldn't get to her by startle responses.

"My client's security is paramount. She is not my sole client. I have a reputation to uphold, and I've built that reputation on mutual respect and care." She stood. "Am I free to go?" She pressed harder on the emotional responses she needed to leverage. "I need to search for my missing child."

He stood in turn. "You should wait here. You can't enter Orange Quadrant, but the androids are in communication. Their report will come to me first."

"I will be in touch. I am not confident in your androids." She crossed the room and picked up the Baby suit. "This item is property of my company."

"Stay," he repeated. "That place is hazardous. I warn you, do not attempt entry." He advanced quickly around the desk and wrapped his hand around hers.

It reminded her of a moment ago, when she'd comforted herself by wrapping her fingers together.

Reluctantly, Deralka pulled her hand free. "Orange Quadrant has my child. No hazard is a barrier to a mother. If you have no evidence I have violated station regulations, I will be on my way." That had to be the end of her comments.

"People have died attempting entry there."

Something about the law-man reminded her of someone. Someone she had thought she knew very well. An unfamiliar sensation crawled from the ruffles in her featherings into her mind — a misplaced desire to request his assistance.

Not my kind of people.

Deralka kept her jaw tight, against the possibility she might stray into that trap. She unsealed the door to Calum's office and strode through with only a minor issue, when one of the Baby suit arms caught on the entry latch. The green-zone androids watched impassively as she marched down the walkway alongside their open workspace. The further she walked, the greater her unease grew. She paused at the exit to the Security Office and looked back. The odd sensation of stretching didn't fit with the effects of the relatively mild station gravity.

She forced herself to move on.

She pulled up the sector maps, found the restaurant again, zoomed to the interior map of the place, and found the service areas that backed onto the Orange barrier. She couldn't possibly follow Girl into a vent. But the underfloor area. That could be accessible.

Then it came to her, as the stretching sensation pulled at her relentlessly.

Attachment.
She'd attached to him. To a human. To a law-man, no less.
This could become inconvenient.

81

11

ARTIFACTS

G IRL WONDERED if this story that Caretaker needed her to identify something could possibly be true. Grown-ups had a tendency to think they could flatter children into compliance. Even so, she didn't know where to go in this maze of corridors. If Caretaker would keep its distance, she could see that it might be helpful, whether it intended to be or not.

"Let's go," she said. "But you go first."

Caretaker nodded, then unfolded its spindly legs and stood up. It turned around — not taking even one step closer to Girl — and began to walk back where it came from.

Girl patted Ashoka with the tips of her fronds, where they wrapped around her little passenger. The cretzina snuggled tightly to Girl's back and smoothed her feathers down in contentment. Girl popped up a pair of eyes to watch Ashoka, then hinged her feet for quick-walking and followed Caretaker.

Rocked by the swaying of Girl's body, Ashoka drifted to sleep, recovering from her fright and her dangerous excursion.

Caretaker's path led past interior hatchways and simple doors. Some of the doors stood open, but the rooms within had no lights. It seemed to be true, that Caretaker lived alone here in this Orange place. Except that the place was done up in yellow and grey.

"Why is it called orange when it isn't?" she asked.

Caretaker paused and turned its head. She could see the curve of one eye as it spoke. "They are confused, if they call this sector Orange. This is the Light sector."

"Why is it light? It's not as light as in the mall or on the docking ring."

This time, when Caretaker stopped, it turned all the way round and put one hand on its chest and gazed down at Girl with great solemnity. "It is not called that for the degree of illumination cast by the lamps here. It is named for that inner illumination that frees the minds of those who think. Enlightenment."

Girl pondered the big human words. "Oh."

Caretaker took in her answer, then asked a question. "Are you an adult, Girl? Or are you a child of your species?"

Girl didn't like to call herself a child. Yesterday, maybe, when she was Boy. Today, everything felt different, but she didn't feel like an adult. Not yet. She wasn't even sure she should be calling herself 'Girl.'

"I'm not sure," she replied. "I think I am neither one. I am an in-between."

It was Caretaker's turn to say, "Oh."

As they began to walk again, Girl turned over the ideas that Caretaker had been trying to talk about. He'd said there could be light inside your head, only it wasn't light. Did Girl have a light inside her head? Did Caretaker? Did Ashoka?

Did an android have a light inside its head?

"How do you know if you are enlightened?" Girl asked next.

Caretaker slowed and moved to one side of the passageway. When Girl had caught up, it continued walking, at just the right pace for her to keep up. She thought it would answer her question then, but it didn't say a word.

"So what's the answer? How do I know if I have a light in my head?"

"I gave you my answer, moments ago."

"You didn't —"

Girl's fronds twitched at the puzzle. All Caretaker had done was to slow down and let Girl walk beside it, instead of leaving her to follow, like a typical adult would do. Nicer adults, though, like the ones she vaguely remembered, thought about what she needed, and moved at her pace, not theirs. They could see into the minds of others, even children.

"Ohhhh."

"Also, by looking upon you, I see one very strong sign of enlightenment with you."

She lifted her sessile eyes close to their curtain of feathers, to watch where its eyes pointed. It had its eyes pointed behind hers, but not so far back that it could be watching her trailing fronds. No, Caretaker was looking at Ashoka.

"I'm *enlightened* because of Ashoka?"

"What have you done for Ashoka?" Its words came as a counterpoint to the sound of its footsteps, steady and sure.

"I came to rescue her, and to keep her company."

"Just so," it said, and its mouth made a very human-looking smile. "A sentient being recognizes itself and knows its needs. An enlightened one recognizes the needs of the other." Then, "Here we are."

It pushed on a nondescript yellow-grey panel, which became a door, and Caretaker led the way through.

The room beyond the door smelled different than the corridor. For one, this room had not even a speck of dust in it. Behind her, Girl watched an array of tiny bots fling themselves into the air around the door, scooping up every bit of dust that had swirled in after them. They vanished as quickly as they had appeared, seeming to melt themselves right into the walls.

Caretaker chuckled. "Come along, Girl-or-Maybe-Not. We are nearly there, but not quite."

Girl/Not Girl returned her attention to Caretaker. "Where are we going?"

The other thing about this room was that it was full of interesting objects. Girl/Not Girl would have liked to explore this room, with those buttons that needed pressed, those sliders needing to be pushed from one end of a slot to another. She wanted to feel if the sliders went *click-click-click* as they moved along. Did the symbols alongside the groove indicate words or numbers?

All the objects were set up on low tables arranged precisely to fill the room with just enough space for Caretaker to pass by without touching anything. The things were a little too close for Girl/Not Girl to ignore, though. Even without meaning to, she extended her fronds and brushed them lightly over the surface of the nearest machine. No trace of electricity, or poison, or even etheric energy tickled at her fingertips, though some of the devices reminded her of the ancient-tech units back on her family's ship.

"Don't touch anything," Caretaker said, in a smooth, calm voice.

Did that mean it didn't really care? Or was it trying to treat her like a grown-up? She stretched one frond underneath the table beside her, still detecting no signs of energy flows.

"Does it matter?" she said. "Everything is off, right?"

"One never knows," Caretaker replied. "One never knows."

She'd heard that phrase before. It reminded her sometimes things happened that one couldn't be prepared for. "What are all these things?"

"They are my artifacts."

"Arty facts?" Girl/Not Girl did not perceive these objects as works of art.

"Artifacts. These are the things that I take care of."

Not art, I think he means old things. "Oh. Are they very old, then?"

"Very, very old."

"Are you very, very old, too, Caretaker?"

Caretaker did not reply to that.

A new door opened at the far end of the room, and Girl/Not Girl followed Caretaker through with a wistful sense of loss. The door closed on the wonderful artifacts. Beyond the door lay another boring, empty corridor.

Ashoka stirred in her sleep and made grumbly, hungry noises from Girl/Not Girl's back. She wished she'd brought some of Ashoka's food pellets. She wished she'd brought Ashoka's baby-bed containment. Carrying the cretzina was hard work in human-level gravity. Most of Ashoka's mass, like Girl/Not Girl's, resided in her exoskeleton, and the linkages of her fronds, and her weapons. Darrougha had a well-deserved reputation for harshness, but her world compensated by gifting its denizens with a wealth of metals and stone and crystal. The life of her homeworld relished in those treasures, making them a part of their living selves.

It had been an awful surprise to fly forth from the homeworld, to meet aliens with weak fleshy bodies who relied on machinery for so much. They didn't taste good, and it was too easy to kill them, so there wasn't any fun in battling them, but they so wanted to battle all the time. Humans had a way of rallying allies to them, so they united long enough to drive the Darroughons back to their home planet.

After that success, humans became arrogant. Even though their allies went home to mind their own business, humans decided they should descend upon defeated Darrougha and claim the planet's rich deposits of compressed-carbon crystals and similar glittery valuables. Darroughons taught them this was a bad idea, but it came to humans as an unwanted lesson. They retreated back to their orbiting command post and built a wall of watchers around Darrougha. They declared that if they couldn't have those treasures, then no one could. Darrougha became proscribed, and the people became prisoners on their own world.

Or so the humans believed.

Space is big.

The space around a large planet with a dynamic magnetosphere revolving about a red dwarf star with a penchant for sudden solar storms made patrolling for escapees difficult. After a few lifetimes of determined technological development, most Darroughons found their prison to be more of a safe haven, a world they cherished for themselves and their attachments. But a few — a bare, adventurous few — ventured out, leveraging what they'd learned of themselves, of the humans, of conflict and avoidance.

Girl/Not Girl knew those lessons by heart. Someone had drilled them into her day and night and twilight, even though the changes she was going through just now left her mind fuzzy on just who that had been. It would come to her. Everything would be all right; she'd been promised that. If only she could settle, she could sort out her confused thoughts and muddled feelings. She had changed twice today, already. When would it stop?

12

CHANGE

Deralka, too, worried about the changes Girl was going through just now. A child needs a mother during such times, but what could she have done? The transaction had been pre-arranged, everything went exactly according to plan.

Or had it?

The cretzina should have been sleeping, happy in a little dream induced by the medicine she'd put into the food that morning.

But it had been Girl — newly Girl and more herself than ever — who had fed the cretzina. Now that she thought of it, Deralka recalled seeing both food containers sitting out when they left the room. She had most certainly tidied everything away before sleeping last night.

Girl had switched the food.

Why? Out of mischief? Boy, not so very long ago, had been quite the mischievous scamp, more likely to disassemble a new toy than to play with it as intended.

Deralka hurried, making her way back to the scene of disaster, her hearts full of worry for Girl, with a little anger simmering underneath. Girl knew the importance of a smooth transaction. She knew that everything in their future rode on this one exchange. The dream Deralka held so dear hung on a thread of circumstance, with each step necessary for its achievement.

And now that thread had snapped, and now what mattered was Girl, lost in those inaccessible channels within the station superstructure, her attachment broken.

As she walked, Deralka wriggled one frond free of the arm it helped control. She would have to be more careful using that portion of the skinsuit, but it could not be helped. For a few moments, she disengaged part of her emotive connections to the skinsuit, so that she wouldn't disrupt its progress down the length of the Mall. Within the suit, she had light enough for the task of adding a few specialized sensors and operating codes to the tip of the frond. Then, without thinking further on it, she threaded that frond through the teeth of her biting jaw and snapped down, severing the end with its new sensors and capabilities. The remaining stub was just long enough to lift the squirming bit of feathery intelligence up through the torso towards the mouth of the skinsuit.

Ignoring her approach, the two orange-keyed security androids stood at attention in front of the huge hatchway leading to the Orange Sector. As Deralka drew close, the frond-tip squiggled into the skinsuit throat. At just the right moment, the tendril vibrated at the back of her skinsuit's mouth, and she coughed — a deep, gut-wrenching paroxysm that flung that bit of herself past the androids, nearly to the edge of the sector wall.

The security androids made no comforting remarks. After all the time she'd spent among humans, the lack of empathy left her lost. A human person would ask her —

"Are you all right?"

She turned, wiping the mouth of the skinsuit, working herself back into full interconnection, so that she could manage its responses more realistically. The restaurant's maître d' stood behind her, his face filled with concern. His broad shape all but blocked her view down the mall.

Why did I attach to that nosy law-man and not to this helpful person? she wondered.

"No, I'm sorry," she told him, using the best of her sorrowful facial expressions. "I'm very upset, and I'm afraid it's making me also not feel well. My little girl's in there," she said, pointing to the giant hatch.

From the corner of her eye, she watched her frond-tip squiggle along the wall and begin the arduous journey up along the rim of the hatchway. It would be a little while before it reached the hatch.

"Would you like to come inside? I can set you a table. It is a better place to wait, wouldn't you say? Our security director is extremely able. I'm sure everything will be fine, soon." He spread an arm towards the restaurant entry.

Deralka bent her head in that little nodding motion she had mastered and let warm tears run out of her skinsuit's eyes. She could clean up the mess later. The maître d' held out his elbow, and she tucked one hand into the loop it made next to that enormous torso of his. Together, they walked back into the restaurant.

He seated her at a table by the window and brought her another of the drinks she'd requested so long, long ago, when she had been about to consummate her final deal.

"Thank you," Deralka told him.

He bobbed his head in the way that meant she had pleased him by accepting his kindness. Then he made the rounds of his other guests, each engaged in their own private and important negotiations.

Deralka's window faced the mall walkway, and she'd taken the chair that would give her a view of the hatchway. With some surprise, she noted that her specially-equipped frond had already made it nearly to the top edge of the hatchway. Within the skinsuit, she hurriedly thrust the broken-off frond into the proper arm-tube to connect directly with her device, so that she could do more than sense the frond's tactile inputs as it traveled. Those thermal and visual sensors were valuable, and it would take significant time to regrow those precious fingertips, so she wanted to get as much information as she could from the sacrifice.

By the time she had full access to that thin little datastream, there was little time to test the encryption space. The tendril had already reached the open hatch. It inchwormed up the last bit of vertical wall, using every bit of microstatic charge to hold itself fast.

To any observer, Deralka would have seemed the very prototype of the anxious soul waiting for tragic news. She sat gazing towards the place she'd lost her child, her eyes misty and unfocused. From time to time, she lifted to her lips the sweet, fruity drink the maître d' had brought for her, but she barely drank. The picture she created should evoke sympathy without suspicion.

Within her disguise, Deralka focused on the progress of her little biological spybot. Small as it was, the thing could hardly travel at the rate Girl would have gone — let alone at the speed of an alarmed cretzina. On the other hand, its slow progress allowed her to collect sensor data. Here, there was a thread of white feathering from the cretzina — so, proof that she had taken the correct direction on entering the vent. Further along, she spotted distinctive scratching in the surface of the duct. Girl had used her foot-talons, extended just slightly, to keep her grip secure on the slippery metal. She must have been scuttling quickly, undoubtedly hurrying to catch up to ... what had she named the cretzina? Ashoka, yes, that was it.

The frond-tip inched its way along, quicker than one might expect for a creature with no arms, no legs, and very little brain. It ran like a millipede, twisting itself in curving arcs while swirling its featherings like miniature legs. For a desperation trick, this scheme had proved surprisingly practical. Deralka sipped sugar-water to calm her optimism. She'd read about someone doing this, long ago, during the war, but she'd always thought the story apocryphal.

She'd downed about half the drink when something new appeared. The image formed by the sensors she'd placed on the tendril resolved in clarity as the frond-tip worked its way closer. At one side of the vent, a sealed hatchway appeared. It looked for all the world like a miniature version of the great hatchway in front of her. She made the frond-tip stop and inspect the tiny hatch thoroughly. Why a secure pressure-hatch inside an air vent?

Aha.

Behind the miniature hatch, it becomes Orange Quadrant.

At one time, the station sectors must have connected through those hatches, so that air pressure would equalize across the station. Deralka allowed herself a moment's relief. Girl's skinsuit might be trapped over there in Orange Quadrant, but Girl herself would be somewhere here, in this vent system. She just needed the time and the patience to seek her out.

The frond-tip moved onward at her request, but it seemed reluctant. It strolled along, rather than running, and cast its sensors from side to side, searching and searching for something that wasn't there.

Deralka put down her glass and told the frond-tip to stop.

It was right.

There were no signs here of either Ashoka or Girl. No dropped featherings. No scratches on the metal. With a growing sense of foreboding, she watched intently for those signs as the frond-tip made its way back to the sealed vent-hatch.

However they had done it, the cretzina and her child had passed through that hatch.

Calum was right. Orange Quadrant had her child.

Not for long, she vowed.

13

MOTHER

DERALKA RAISED A HAND to notify the waitperson not to disturb her table, that she needed to visit the relief facilities. These, she knew, were situated close to the sector wall, with one designated for privacy-seeking individuals. She was pleased to find the space unoccupied — but it might not remain empty for long. Moving with deliberation, quelling her haste and anger, Deralka closed herself into one of the relief cubicles. It looked to be designed for a relatively large variety of humanoid.

She positioned her skinsuit on the little chair-like thing, but kept the cover down. The hoses and air blasters underneath had a disturbing configuration, as if the chair prepared to do battle with any creature that approached it. Then, faster than she'd ever done before, Deralka peeled herself out of the skinsuit.

She wasted no time enjoying the freedom of motion. With utmost care, she re-sealed the seams and positioned the skinsuit in such a way that it appeared to be holding its head in its hands. She waited for the programming to kick in. Soon enough, the skinsuit emitted a soft sound and its shoulders went up and down. She pulled an extra video sensor from her tool bag and slapped it to the wall, where it could detect anyone trying to interfere. The skinsuit had a self-defense mode she could switch on remotely, but she hoped not to have to activate it. There could be unpleasant consequences.

She retrieved her device and checked to be sure there were no spybots doing anything unexpected in the vicinity. Then she reactivated the feed for the visual spybots — did patrons know that their host had them on record in the relief area of the restaurant? Possibly. So many sensitive transactions were conducted in this establishment, one never knew where a conflict might arise.

Housekeeping tasks complete, Deralka unsheathed her talons. As easily as a chef cutting tea cakes – an image came to mind, of the treats flying across the room when Calum's team invaded her client meeting — she sliced three sides of a square hole in the metal sheathing of the floor.

In moments, she had folded back the trap-door she'd created and slipped underneath, into the service space below the floor. Taking care to line up the edges, she pulled the cover back into place. Then she began to work her way downwards, to the main accessways for utilities and materials that any well-functioning ship would have close by the actively-used areas, but well out of sight.

By the time she stood on top of the cable network, looking out at tubes and pipes and structures of even more opaque function, Deralka had every one of her talons fully-exposed, ready for battle. When she stepped onto a cable-sheath, she considered a moment, then drew in the foot-talons a little. It wouldn't do to accidentally cut off some important station function. She needed the station working when she retrieved Girl and Ashoka. They would need to depart in a hurry.

A million thoughts fought for attention in Deralka's mind, but she had no time for them. She didn't have time to wonder if the trauma of he-that-had-departed had somehow made Boy change too early. She didn't have time to figure out how she had managed to form an attachment to Calum Schoonover. She certainly had no time to think about what she would do next, with her investment shot, her merchandise gone, and Girl almost certainly exposed as the most feared monster ever encountered in human space.

She worked her way along the interstices of the utility spaces, sidling along cables, dodging protrusions from transport tubes, gripping with crystal-edged talons the smooth surfaces that hung over drop-channels to nowhere.

An eerie glow began to suffuse the space. At first, she guessed she was adapting to the dimness, with the modicum of safety lighting provided for those rare occasions a human, not an android, came down here for a maintenance task. The glow increased as she went along, until she came to the source.

The barrier between sectors had its demarcation here — an orange-gold sheet of light spread from the upper surface of the accessway down to the lowest. Perhaps this was merely a warning light-show. She advanced to it and extended one frond, enough to brush the seeming surface with her featherings.

Nothing happened.

She stretched the frond further, and it passed through the light without interference.

So, it was merely a show, to remind maintenance crew, whether living or mechanical, to keep out.

Deralka stepped through the curtain, alert to any probing from the vicinity of the light emitters.

She made it barely a few body-lengths before she heard the sound. Metallic scuttling sounds echoed around her. She tucked a couple of eyes down safe, just in case, and extended the rest, soaking in every wavelength she could access. Heat signatures glowed around her, not the pulsating heat of living beings, but the steady gleam of electric motors.

Androids? Here?

She flexed her fronds and scuttled onward.

Then she saw them. Not androids, but robots built like herself, with powerful graspers and long arms to swing from point to point in this jungle of cables and pipes. They each bore the orange swirl of the forbidden zone.

"I've come for my child!" she shouted. "Get out of my way!"

They descended with limbs extended, sharp-edged tools gleaming at the extremities. Conversation did not seem to be part of their repertoire.

She drew her fronds inward, compressing her impulse bands while flicking the point-guards free. The hard plasteel covers clicked and clattered on pipes and conduit as they twirled in the Coriolis force and tumbled towards the station's outer hull. The sounds diverted the attention of the robots, enough to give her a second to scuttle with her back to a tall box-shaped structure. She arranged herself alongside parallel lengths of piping too narrow for those robots to squeeze between. They would have to come at her one at a time.

Had they ever encountered a Darroughon?

Not likely.

Did they have access to databanks that might inform their actions?

Perhaps.

She would have to move quickly.

Make the first move, Deralka. Draw them to you.

Her own father's voice whispered in her memory, from days on the hunt in the forests of Darrougha.

She stretched one frond to a bright orange tube running overhead, and sliced through it in one quick motion. A cool, clear fluid sprayed into the space between her and her new-found enemies.

One sprang upwards, deploying repair tools. Another surged beneath that first, towards Deralka.

One long metal arm ended in graspers, the inner edges of each jaw grooved to improve gripping.

The other robotic arm flashed with a blade as bright as Deralka's talons.

Come along, then, closer, closer.

Now.

She released two fronds. They unfurled with a crack that echoed from the curves and smooth surfaces, as if a projectile weapon had been unleashed. The right frond snapped over the claw-like grasper, encircling it in steel and feathers, tightening almost instantly to close those teeth together. The left frond deployed paired talons that severed the robot's other limb at the base of its blade. Without hesitating, before the robot could react, that frond whipped over the machine's upper surface and sliced the captured claw free of its support. As she drew the cutting frond back, she deployed its talons, scraping the robot's forward sensors into oblivion. At the same time, the frond grasping the detached claw uncoiled, flinging the useless claw into the robot's body, timing the spin so that the sharp edges penetrated its thick plasteel housing.

The repair robot dropped, replacing its companion out of the approach path. As the new attacker rotated towards her, she detected the heat signature of an energy weapon — not exactly a weapon, but the laser tool it had been using for repairs. Regardless, the beam posed a deadly hazard.

Deralka spun in place, presenting the base of her carapace and her all-but-indestructible legs. In the same move, she compressed her fronds against the surface at her back. She barely felt the heat from the laser, but it was enough to gauge the robot's movement and position. In unison, her fronds pushed off, propelling her towards her opponent, all four legs fully extended, locked in position, toe-knives deployed. She'd given herself a spin around her own vertical axis of about a revolution per second. When she struck the laser-wielding robot, her toes sliced through its extended limb first, then the one it held back — or held ready for a fresh attack — then carved four long arcs through the machine's housing. She recognized the electric surge of shredded cables.

She halted her spin by grabbing onto the nearest pipe, snagged the laser tool from the disabled robot's grip, then flung herself back to her defensive position.

The next robot in the queue hesitated. Probably, it was downloading data.

Deralka aligned her fronds, tested her legs. She'd taken no damage.

Time to go.

Now, moving into attack configuration, she sprang from her legs and deployed all ten of her arms, somersaulting over the hesitant robot, slicing it from above as she passed over. Another detached limb clanked as it fell. She was already disassembling the next robot in the queue. The one behind that tried to retreat, but she caught it by the legs, fried its motive unit with the laser tool, and pushed it backwards, to commiserate with its disabled companions.

By then, the last few robots were in full flight. They dodged and leaped from pipe to cable to channel housing, chittering at one another or calling for help.

She pursued them in silence.

One she caught mid-leap between supporting beams. The next-to-last fell under her knives when the available passage narrowed and its companion made it to the tunnel first.

The last demonstrated determination enough for a young Darroughon — though not the skills of an experienced hunter. When the channel space opened wide, and a side-path presented itself, she feinted an intention to take the alternate route. When her prey paused, confused by her failure to follow, she sprang at it, piercing its back with her feet and snaring its claw in two fronds and its manipulative arm with another pair.

The rest of her fronds she folded neatly, retracting their talons. She hunkered down on the robot's back like a Darroughon child carried by a parent.

"Now," she ordered. "Take me to your leader."

The machine squealed a message to whatever might be listening, but then carried her on through the underfloor of Orange Quadrant.

14

IDENTITY

"HERE, NOW," said Caretaker. "Let's see just what you are, Girl-who-isn't-one."

Caretaker had led Girl/Not Girl into a new room, this one behind a proper station-type doorway. It wasn't a secret door like the last one. It didn't disappear behind her when Caretaker closed it. The room was cleaner than the corridor, but not as spotless as the artifacts room.

This time, a single large machine nearly filled the room. It had the same squiggly writing on it that the artifacts had, but somehow Girl/Not-Girl knew it didn't belong with them. It wasn't that old.

Girl/Not-Girl did not like that machine. She didn't want to push its buttons or feel the bumpy shapes that showed all over its inner surfaces. Maybe she didn't like it because it was so big. Maybe she didn't like it because Caretaker wanted her to get into it. The machine gave her the feeling it wanted to eat her up.

"I'm not going in there," she told Caretaker. "Nobody's going to eat me. I have to take care of Ashoka."

"But the Delineator is going to read you, not eat you."

"Read me?"

"I built this to help me recognize things. I've seen so much in my life and there's so much I've never seen. You have to understand, when you see too much, you begin to forget what you know and don't know. The Delineator looks at things and tells me what they are."

Caretaker seemed proud of its machine. People, especially humans, tended to be proud of things they should not be proud of, things that were wrong.

"But I'm not a thing. I'm a person." Girl/Not Girl backed away. She looked at the door, hoping it would open for her.

"It's perfectly safe."

"Prove it." Girl had an idea, a perfect idea. "You get in. Make the Delineator read you."

"Me? But I know what I am."

"I don't."

Girl curled most of her fronds around Ashoka, but she kept two out, so she could wave them around, like people waved their arms when they talked.

"I told you, I'm the Caretaker."

"And I told you. I'm Girl."

"But you're not."

Well, there was that. Girl wondered if the machine could tell her what she was now, herself. She wondered if it could tell her if she would keep on changing all the time now, or what? Still, she wanted to win the argument, first, and find out what Caretaker was.

"That doesn't matter. You have to prove it's safe. And I'll believe you if you make it read you first."

"Huh." Caretaker sounded like it couldn't think of the right words to argue with her.

It went over to the machine and ran its fingers over the curving entry to the open shape. The inside of the machine was like a little room with two bumpily walls and a floor and a ceiling.

"Look," Caretaker said. "It's not going to eat you up. See? There's no door to shut you in. See?"

Caretaker stepped over the threshold and walked right through the machine's open space. Its head went out of sight above the top of the opening on the other side, but then it bent down and waved at her from over there. Girl strolled up, looking at the control panel to the machine with four eyes and watching Caretaker with the rest.

The GO button was labeled in squiggle, but it was pretty obvious.

Caretaker stepped back into the chamber, to make its way back to her.

She pressed GO.

The whole machine began to hum, very, very softly. Maybe a human wouldn't have heard it. A rainbow of colors chased themselves around the inner surfaces of the reading chamber. Caretaker stopped, and stayed still, rubbing a finger over one ear as if the sound bothered it a little.

That was all.

The noise stopped, the colors went plain grey again, and Caretaker stepped out.

"I told you not to press buttons," it said. It didn't seem angry. It rubbed its head and blinked several times. "It does feel strange," it admitted. "I'm not hurt, though. You see? It's harmless."

The machine made a soft pinging noise and a tall monitor screen lit up above the control panel. To Girl/Not-Girl's disappointment, the writing was in that useless squiggle writing. She'd never seen anything like that, so even if she'd had her device with her, she wouldn't have made sense of it.

"Here," Caretaker said. "You probably can't read this." It pushed a slider switch with two fingers, stopping it at a particular position.

Suddenly, a new voice echoed in the room, though, to Girl/Not-Girl's ears, the voice sounded very like Caretaker's.

The voice began to go on about The Subject. It rattled off lots of words that didn't make sense to Girl/Not-Girl. It never said anything scary, though. None of the strange things the machine told her about Caretaker made her want to run away. The machine said Caretaker was endangered, using a word that Girl/Not Girl knew well, one that often applied to the animals she'd met. She felt a little sorry for Caretaker then, because probably this meant it had no one to take care of itself.

"Well. I don't understand a lot of that. Can you send it to my device, when I get it back? I have a lot of words to look up, I think."

"Hmm. Maybe. I'm not sure my machine can talk to your ... device." Caretaker flicked another switch, and the message screen went dark. "I saved the data, though. There were things it said that I ... hmm ... want to look up, too."

Maybe Caretaker should have done this a while ago. It seemed to have forgotten about more than its artifacts. Girl/Not-Girl hoped this news wouldn't make it sad, to remember it was *endangered*.

"Your turn," said Caretaker.

She still didn't like it, but Caretaker had done what she asked. Even if only because she pulled a trick. Its request seemed fair, now.

Girl/Not Girl took a step forward, then stopped. Very gently, she scooped several fronds under Ashoka and lifted her out, to set her safely off to one side.

"You leave her be," she warned Caretaker. "Ashoka is cute, but she can be dangerous, too."

"I will keep that in mind."

Girl/Not-Girl scuttled up into the chamber before she could change her mind. It was like a transaction, right? They had made an agreement, and she needed to fulfill her part of the bargain. That didn't mean she liked it when the hum started up, all around her now, vibrating her ears and even ruffling her feathers. The racing colors, though, those were fun. She wanted to chase them round and round the chamber, but she knew the gravity wasn't light enough to make that possible.

She was disappointed when the light show ended, but she didn't miss the hum.

Hurrying to Caretaker's side, she waited impatiently for the pinging sound, then reached up and slid the slider just to where he'd placed it. Another screenful of incomprehensible text lit up above her, and then Caretaker's voice began to recite the history of the Darroughons, their biology, and their social structures. Girl/Not-Girl listened attentively. She hadn't realized, being a child, how much attachment drove the way things worked at home. She understood something that had never made sense to her before, that most people — Darroughons, humans, so many species — preferred to stay at home on their own planets. For her own people, going out among the stars could only work if they traveled within the web of their attachments.

"That's very interesting," she said, feeling the deep sounds in her voice that would tell a fellow Darroughon just how impressed she was with Caretaker's machine.

"You are even more interesting than I expected," Caretaker said. "Why have you come here with your little animal, then?"

"We came because somebody wanted it," she said. "A person who wants an interesting creature calls on us and we go find what they want and bring it. We also teach them how to care for and to be safe with the creatures. Some of them are dangerous, like Ashoka."

"That doesn't seem fair," Caretaker said.

"Why not?" Girl/Not-Girl felt offended. *We do everything right*, she thought.

"Just one person gets to see and understand the interesting creature? That hardly seems ... would 'efficient' be a better word than 'fair'?"

"What do you mean?"

"You have one rare creature and one person sees it. What if you made it so many persons could see and learn about the rare creature?"

Girl/Not-Girl was still annoyed that Caretaker would criticize her family's business. "Your machine didn't tell me if I'm a girl or not. It told you you're an endangered species."

"I don't think my machine is that smart. It did tell me that your species changes genders. How many genders does your species have?"

"Two, like humans." Girl/Not-Girl scuttled back to Ashoka and settled the cretzina safely onto her back again. The question bothered her. "I think. I don't know. Changing is weird. I feel all crumbly inside and I want it to stop."

Caretaker knelt down in front of Girl/Not-Girl, so its eyes were not so very much higher than hers, as they stretched up on their stalks. "Young, growing creatures of all species change in many ways as they mature. Only you will know what you are when you are grown. Like me, you must learn to be yourself, whatever that may turn out to be."

Its words didn't heal the crunchy, achy feeling inside her, but they made her mind see a little more clearly.

"So, what now, Caretaker? You said you found something."

It shifted back to its feet, once more towering over her. "Yes, my androids found something interesting. And you are very interesting. So I think maybe you belong together."

"What is it?" Not-Girl asked as she followed Caretaker out of the Delineator Room.

"I'm not sure," Caretaker said. "I haven't seen anything like it before."

Its strides began to lengthen, and Girl had to scuttle hard to keep up.

"You're going too fast," she called out.

It looked back, then slowed to match her pace again.

"I am forgetting myself. I am used to being on my own, you see."

"Except for all the androids."

"Yes, except for all my and — Oh!" Its face changed expressions.

She guessed that it was being surprised. It held its head as if listening to something.

"What's the matter?"

Uncertain, she wondered if she should turn around and flee while Caretaker was distracted. She had more than half decided to do just that when it stopped listening. Caretaker must have had something like a device to give it information.

"Speaking of my androids, they have found another something."

"Oh, what?"

"They are very confused. But I think it is another something that you can explain to me."

"Oh, all right."

Somehow, having Caretaker need her advice made it less frightening again.

"But don't go running off. I can't rush while carrying Ashoka. She needs to stay calm."

Caretaker nodded. It seemed serious and respectful, like the maître d' at the restaurant, even though Caretaker was half the width of the average human and the maître d' was easily twice a human wide.

15

KNOWLEDGE

N OT-GIRL DID GEOMETRY in her head as she followed Caretaker down the narrow corridor. They had walked a long way spinward, then wandered through some rooms, and now they were walking antispinward. She could tell by the way the false gravity shifted each step just a microscopic amount. She tried to estimate the distance she and Ashoka had traveled inside the vent passageway.

"We're going to where the big hatch is, aren't we?"

"Well, not quite that far. We're going where the first thing is: a workroom that's close to the hatch. Is that all right?" It looked down at her with that being-kind expression. "Are you frightened of the big hatch, girl-who-is-not-one?"

"No, I'm not scared."

"Good."

Now that she knew where they were going, it didn't seem so far. When Caretaker finally pressed on another anonymous wall segment and beckoned her to follow, Not-Girl hardly even considered being surprised.

This new room didn't have any more of those artifacts covered with strange squiggly writing. It didn't contain a giant machine designed to be climbed inside of. It had six plain, evenly-spaced walls, each smooth and grey, with yellowish flecks showing under the surface. Several different kinds of chairs occupied the room, in scattered clusters. Some chairs looked soft and comfortable; others looked like their purpose was to keep you from falling asleep. One or two seemed made for something other than a human shape. None were made for a Darroughon.

However, on a smallish chair at the far side of the room sat an odd-looking human boy. He stared blankly at the nearest wall and didn't even flinch when the door snicked open and snacked closed.

"Who's that? Why is he here?" Not-Girl scuttled closer and looked up into the boy's face. Embarrassment crinkled the curves of her fronds. "Oh. Is this all you found?" Girl's featherings twitched in annoyance.

Caretaker had made such a fuss over a skinsuit? Why hadn't it just stuffed the Boy suit into the Delineator?

"Indeed. Is it not yours?" It seemed to be feeling very clever.

"Of course it is. I know you know it's mine. I don't like being fooled, Caretaker."

"But it's so interesting! I wanted to talk to you about it. Would you have come otherwise?"

"Maybe."

She wasn't sure of that, though. If it had said, "Come with me, I want to talk to you," wouldn't that have made her run away? That was the kind of thing law-men said, and she'd been warned about that plenty of times.

"What's it for?" Caretaker did seem genuinely interested in the skinsuit, in the same way it was interested in reading what the Delineator told about her.

Girl knew she wasn't supposed to share Darroughon technology — not even with someone she felt as close to as Caretaker. Then again, why did she feel so close to Caretaker? It wasn't a Darroughon. It wasn't even a human, according to the Delineator. If she'd understood what it was saying, Caretaker made itself look like other species, so it could talk with them. And stay safe.

"It's so I can be like you." That wouldn't give away any secrets, not at this point, now that Caretaker had seen her. "It makes me look like a human, so I can go around them and not scare them."

"Can you tell me how it works?"

Girl curled her fronds tight. That was treading too close.

"No," she said. "But I can show you how I use it."

With precise efficiency, as she'd been taught, Not-Girl released the seals and slipped the seams open. She remembered when the human had helped open the Baby suit that Ashoka was riding in. Like that eager customer, Caretaker seemed undisturbed by the sight of a human body opened up like a piece of baggage.

Not-Girl lifted Ashoka from her back, and settled her on one of the nice comfy chairs. Curious, Ashoka ran her fronds over the surface, then she twirled around a couple of times before settling down to watch Girl.

"If you could steady it for me," she said, "Just by holding the legs still."

Caretaker obliged, bending down to grasp the suit by its tubular legs while she scurried up to the platform within.

"See? Here's where my arms go. I can put as many as five into each of these tubes here, though usually I just put four, so I can have a few free to play with inside. Sometimes I need to adjust the controls — here, see?"

She brushed her fingertips over the control panel and the suit's eyes, pointed at the ceiling in its tipped-back head, blinked slowly and made wrinkles at their corners, like the Boy was thinking hard about something.

"There's lots of connections for sensors and actuators. It's fun walking around on two legs. It feels dangerous, but the balance systems have a good design. I've only had it fall over a few times."

"You must be very clever to manage all this. I need to make an adjustment once every hundred years or so, and then I need to take plenty of time to get used to it."

"Does it bother you, to change?"

It lifted its shoulders in a very human-like shrug. "Change is part of life. One must welcome it. I am still myself, always, but now I can speak to people like yourself, which my older shapes could not have done."

"Oh."

Not-Girl tasted around the edges of those ideas. If Caretaker was happy with being changed, why hide in this Orange place? She didn't want to hurt its feelings, though.

Caretaker seemed to be having the same thoughts about her. "But why do you need a skinsuit? You can speak the human language well enough without it."

"Didn't you listen to your Delineator? It isn't the way we talk that humans don't like; it's the way we look. And some things we did back when we first met them." She didn't like talking about those things, but Caretaker deserved to know. She felt strangely connected to it, like there was an electric cable running between them. "It wasn't our fault. We didn't understand how weak they were."

"But you understand now."

"Yes, but why should they believe us? We are still dangerous." She lifted one frond and extended one of the talons she'd used to cut away the seals on the vent hatch. It glittered under the lights. "They can't trust us. We can't show that much of ourselves."

"Yet."

"No, not yet. Maybe someday. We have to find a way for them to get used to us, somehow." Its understanding made her bold. "But you're not scary at all. You're nice, and you look nice, too. Why are you hiding? Why do you need the scary android guards?"

Caretaker folded its long, bony legs and settled down in the stiff, uncomfortable-looking chair next to Ashoka's comfy one. With a single golden finger, it soothed the topmost riffling feathers of Ashoka's back. "It's not in my nature to be threatening, so I have had to enlist the help of the androids. It is the things I protect that are dangerous, little one, not myself. Remember the room with the artifacts?"

"'Don't touch', you said. I didn't, though."

"Not everyone can listen to such advice. I've gathered here all the dangerous items that once could be found throughout Delphi Station." Caretaker made its almost-human smile. "I wonder what the current occupants would think of the people they call 'Delphians'? At any rate, I continue to collect their tools and the tools of their predecessors. I protect the humans and their guests by keeping these things secret. Do you see?"

"You're like me, then. If you show too much, it could hurt people."

Caretaker nodded. "It's all right to remain behind a shield, whether for your own protection or for another's."

She would have to think about that. "But who are the Delphians?"

"The builders of this place." It glanced at the Boy suit. "They were rather more like your people than humans might want to know.

Surprised, Not-Girl sad, "I thought you built it."

"No, no, I came as a visitor, just like you. I settled here when the station drifted solitary and abandoned. It reminded me of myself, you see. Alone and full of secrets. I hadn't the heart to leave it behind when someone wanted to make it useful again. I wouldn't want these wonderful things to be lost, but the humans aren't ready for them."

"Not yet."

"That's right. You don't need to leave if you don't want to," Caretaker said. "Though it seems you want to."

Not-Girl paused. "I like it here. I like you. But I think there's someplace I need to be. I need to figure that out, first."

"Does this have something to do with what you are feeling?"

Caretaker made a little gesture with its hand, and one wall became a screen that was so clear for an instant she thought it was a window. Part of the view was blocked by the backs of orange-zone guards, so Girl figured the sensor for that viewscreen was somewhere on the giant hatch. Beyond the guards stood that law-man who'd interrupted the client meeting. He held a big huge weapon in both hands, one she'd seen in pictures, and he waved it threateningly.

"Surrender the child!" he shouted. "You have no right to detain a minor! I'll blast my way through if you do not comply. You have five mins, no more, to make your decision."

"Five mins is a very short time for a big choice," Caretaker said mildly. "Also, we have no human children here to take to him."

Not-Girl was busy answering the question she'd been wondering about. How had Caretaker figured out the suit was hers? She understood now — it had used its viewscreen to watch her clamber out of the suit to follow Ashoka.

Now, she needed to get back into the Boy suit. She looked over all the connections she needed to make.

I've never done it by myself before. So I'd better go one step at a time.

The easiest part was the leg connections with her feet, so she started there. Once she got going, the process fell into place.

Step by step, that's it.

Caretaker interrupted her thoughts. "Also, there is the other problem I mentioned."

With another hand gesture, it opened a second window-like screen. This one showed a shiny orange-decorated robot, or maybe a robot-like android, with flexible arms, thick multi-jointed legs, and sensors gleaming on its surfaces. On top of that robot rode a living person, one with long green-grey fronds with bright crystal-edged talons extending from each. It was another one of *her*, a Darroughon, a full-grown one.

Sound screeched from the window, too. Not-Girl adjusted her ears to listen to it. The Darroughon called out, over and over, in the station's language and in her own — the language of Darrougha.

"My child! My child! I'm here for my child!"

She redoubled her efforts to secure herself in the skinsuit.

"You're right," she said. "The man out front thinks I'm a human child, and someone has made him very upset that I'm here. Humans care for their children a lot, even though they are stupid and don't know how to make eggs."

"Indeed. Apparently, Darroughons care about children a lot, too."

"Yes. You're right about that."

Not-Girl reached to collect Ashoka from her comfy chair and placed her in her safe space on Not-Girl's carapace. It was a tight squeeze with the both of them, but she was able to fold herself the rest of the way into the skinsuit. Now, she looked out through those two eyes with five of hers paired to the inputs.

Caretaker was smiling again. Did that mean the same as a human smile, or was it expressing something different, a feeling unique to its own species? She strolled around the room a little, to be sure she had the skinsuit legs hooked in properly.

"If the human with the big gun isn't going to wait very long, I should go out right away. I don't want him to hurt your androids or your artifacts."

"Thank you. You are a good person, whatever your name is."

"I don't have a name. I have to grow up more to get a name."

"You seem very grown up to me," Caretaker said, and Not-Girl's hearts rattled with pleasure.

"Can I come back and see you?"

Suddenly, leaving Caretaker behind became her greatest fear. How would she be able to leave the station, now?

"We will find a way," Caretaker said, and her hearts eased up their rattling "Let me show you to the side exit."

She followed it out the same door, then just a little further to a tight-sealed door-hatch that opened to a high, wide space much the size of the open Mall on the other side. One of the orange androids stood waiting at another door-hatch beside the great one.

Not-Girl watched the android work the latches on that small door. *I'm not scared*, she told herself.

Ashoka scritched her little claws across Not-Girl's back, reminding her to be brave. That gave her the strength, the confidence to go out and face the angry law-man and his dangerous weapon.

16

GROWN-UPS

DERALKA STRETCHED all five sessile eyes to watch for signs of movement in these endless, empty corridors. Her captive machine had emerged from the underfloor through a proper hatchway and now moved quickly and steadily. However, though it appeared to be responding to her orders, it did not speak directly. It emitted simple tight-beam radio transmissions, but not in her direction and in an unfamiliar code. Not even her device could translate it. Should she disable this robot now, and proceed on her own?

Who had authority in the Orange Quadrant? The criminals who supposedly managed the station had possession of the sector at the opposite side to the Green Quadrant and its Great Mall. The humans never came here, so what were the options?

On balance, it seemed sensible to save her mental energy for the eventual confrontation. Robots were minions; it remained to be seen who — or what — these minions served.

They bypassed simple doors and sealed hatchways, closed against drifting dust that glittered in the soft, steady lighting. Occasionally, she shouted in human language and in her own, hoping to draw the attention of whatever agents operated here. She also hoped that Girl would hear her calls, that they would draw Girl's attention back to her and restore their attachment.

At a certain point, she began to hear echoes. Every time she called out, something like her own voice called out to her from a distance. The echoes came louder and louder, until the wall opened to become a door, leading into an empty space that resounded with her own voice each time she shouted. One entire wall was filled with a three-dimensional image showing herself and the captured robot. She trained her eyes forward, and summoned data from her device.

She was right.

There were cameras embedded in the walls. She was being observed.

But where was the observer?

Sound burst from another wall in the room. As her captive turned towards the noise, Deralka caught a clear view of Calum, shouting angrily at the guard androids, as he brandished a truly impressive tool. At first glance, it looked like some kind of weapon, but then she recognized it as a laser cutting tool, of the type one might find in a scrapyard for defunct spacecraft. With that thing, he could slice an engine free of its mounting — or beam a hole directly through the hatch itself.

Her hearts beat out a staccato rhythm at the sight of that charming little human facing off against the shining androids. Her thoughts resonated with his demands.

"Release the child! Your time is nearly up! Just one min remaining or so help me I'll fire this thing up! Did you think I couldn't find a tool capable of breaching that hatch? Try me!"

Deralka drove her robot steed onward. A bizarre combination of metal and crystal and feathers and electronics, they barreled through the empty room and out into a broad, high space dominated by the massive, sealed hatchway, the one beyond which Calum even now shouted his challenge, "That's forty secs! I'm counting down now!"

A new sight drove Calum from her mind. Across the entry bay, there stood Girl — or at least Girl's skinsuit — looking up at a long-limbed humanoid with deep orange-gold skin. Deralka's device proclaimed that yes, that was Girl, safely ensconced in her skinsuit.

She reached all ten arms towards them, and cried out, "Girl!"

The tall stranger twisted its head around and looked at her. "Not a girl," it said.

Did it mean itself? Or Girl? Was Girl changed again?

"Boy!" she cried.

"No," the humanoid said. It watched her steadily, seeming taller and taller as the robot carried her closer and closer.

A name floated through Deralka's mind.

A name she'd never heard, never yet given.

Karramana.

She'd given a name once before, but that was for an animal. She remembered the day her father cast her name and forged her first adult attachment, the glorious glow of acceptance, the way it filled her senses with light and joy. She'd broken that bond willingly, but the pain of it still burned in her memory.

Still, it was time. Her child was grown. The name had come to her, and it was her parental duty to give it, not to hold back in fear of a future separation.

"Karramana!" she called, and she sent out her affection, her attachment, and she felt it strike through the skinsuit, to the one within, like a dart trailing a long silver ribbon.

The Boy-shaped skinsuit paused, and turned its head. The gleam of her child's vision shone in its eyes. "In a minute, Mother," it said, or he said, or she said. "I have to go out for a while. I'll be back." Karramana pointed to the golden-orange alien. "This is Caretaker. Be nice. Both of you."

That small side door beside the giant hatch — the same one that had taken in the skinsuit not so very long ago — slid open, and the Boy shape plunged out through it, swinging its arms vigorously. The attachment remained, the gleaming tie between mother and child, and it intertwined with that new attachment, between herself and the human, Calum. There was another tie she perceived in the tangle, as well.

Deralka looked up at the alien humanoid. *Caretaker?* she wondered. *With Karramana attached to this creature and me attached to Calum, we may be here a while.*

It might work out. A successful casino indicated a steady supply of hapless marks upon which she might revive the simple confidence games on which she'd done her early training.

Caretaker flicked its fingers, and the robot settled to the floor. Deralka shook out her fronds and wrenched her foot-talons free of the damaged machine's upper surface. As soon as she clambered down to stand beside it, the robot skittered away as fast as its legs could carry it.

"Pardon the delay. Let us return to my observation room, to see how things go," Caretaker invited her, and she followed it back to that room full of chairs.

•　　•　　•

A thundering blast of fire seared the air overhead as Karramana leapt through the doorway. Above her, the collimated beam of the cutting laser tore at the edge of the giant hatch. Plasteel vaporized to a glowing cloud that drifted upwards, weaving over the tops of the buildings in the mall.

Karramana rushed forward.

"I'm here!" they called out. "I'm all right! It's all all right, now!"

The law-man shut off the laser cutter and pointed it at the decking. One by one, he engaged all three safety levers. Then he reached out one hand and patted the skinsuit on the head.

"I'm glad to see you," he said. "Your mother has been very worried."

"I'll explain everything to her. She won't be angry. She won't be sad."

Everything felt just right, now. Karramana could feel it inside them, like a warm glowing fire. They looked up at the smiling law-man, and wondered at the way he seemed even more worried than Mother had looked.

"That's good." He gave each of the guard androids a glare, as if he wished he'd blasted them with that laser. "Let's go find her."

He held out his hand, and they put their skinsuit hand in his. They could feel the warmth of his real human skin. "My name's Karramana. What's yours?" they asked him.

"My name's Calum Schoonover, but you can just call me Calum, okay?" He began to walk down the mall and they trotted alongside.

I'll need to get a more grown-up skinsuit now, they thought. *Boy was a child and Girl was something in-between, but I'm a grown-up, now. I have a name.*

"I like Schoonover, but Calum is a nice name, too. Did your mother give both of them to you? My mother gave me my name."

They tested the strength of the attachment their mother had just re-formed with them. They had no trouble at all maintaining that one together with the tie to Caretaker and the precious link to Ashoka.

Yes, I'm all grown up now.

"I'm glad to hear it. My longer name was my father's, and he shared it with me."

He swung his arm gently as he walked. They liked the rhythm of it, as it counterpointed the simple two-beat pulse of the human walk.

They looked up at him and wondered, *If I could bond with an endangered alien and a cretzina, would it be possible to attach with a human?*

"Where do you think your mother would have gone? She's not replying to my messages. I would have thought to hear back from her right away." Calum seemed concerned.

"It's okay," Karramana replied. "I can feel her, you know. It's like a special gift. She's all right. Let's look at the hostel first. Yes, I think we should start there."

17

NEVER BEFORE SEEN

"Ah, so all is well, then," said Caretaker. "Will you go now?" It gestured towards the door by which Karramana had departed.

Deralka recognized that this was more of an order than a question.

"I'm afraid I must return the way I came." Suddenly, she realized what she'd forgotten. "Oh, no, the cretzina!"

"The little animal full of knives?" Caretaker had an intriguing smile — probably one it had learned to make, rather than a natural expression. What would this strange humanoid think of her skinsuit's smile? "Your girl-who-is-not-a-girl, she took the Ashoka."

"Oh. You know what it is?"

"Oh, my, yes. The Karramana talked about the Ashoka a great deal."

"If you would, please don't mention it to anyone else. At least for today." If their secret could last long enough to get their ship undocked, it would be enough.

"I am not in the habit of mentioning anything to anybody."

The hidden Caretaker that nobody even knows about.

"I see. Well, I will be on my way. Thank you."

She curled her fronds over her back, and shivered her feathers, knowing full well this creature would not see the gesture as Darroughon respect, but, still, she owed it that much.

Her attachment to Karramana gleamed like a beacon as she retraced the robot's steps to that tidy hatchway and then made her way through the depths to her own untidy hatch in the Restaurant's facilities. She could not regret what she had done to Caretaker's robots, but she resolved to find a way to compensate it for the inevitable expense of replacing or refurbishing them. The Restaurant, too, had suffered damage that would puzzle its owners. She managed to seal the edges of her cutting with the repair robot's laser tool, but the floor still appeared damaged.

It was torture, taking the time to seal herself into her skinsuit properly. She would rather have run through the station as herself, wrap her arms around her child, and say that name over and over.

But she contained those urges and made her way back to the dining room to tell the kindly maître d' that she'd received word her child had been recovered.

On the long walk to the security office, she debated with herself on whether to reach out to her client again.

First, Karramana.

Later, Ashoka.

The cold eyes of the security androids glared at her with something like envy as Deralka strode through their office space, amber hair flowing down her back, her striped fronds working the controls from deep inside her refuge. The moment she stepped through the door to Calum's office,

Karramana leapt down from a chair and threw those strong tubular arms around her waist.

"Mama!"

"Karramana!" The skinsuit was so well-tuned by now, it poured out tears without her operating any controls at all.

Calum stood from behind his desk. He had that same quizzical expression he'd worn so many hours ago, when he pointed his long finger with its impossibly useless claw-nail at the Baby suit while Ashoka's frond-tip pulled the seams open. "What's that?" he said.

Reflexively, Deralka ran her skinsuit's hands over the edges of its seals.

No irregularities.

"Uh-huh." Calum gestured towards the door, in much the same way as Caretaker had done. "Shall we find a private location to talk? I know a place."

•　　　•　　　•

Mother and Director Schoonover talked for a long time, leaning side-by-side at the railing in the Observation Dome, their feet tucked under the toe-rail. Karramana laughed at their stodginess, choosing instead to take off the boring magnetic shoes and soar in the microgravity of the station hub. Below, or above — depending on how they decided to view it — the vast clearsteel dome revealed the galactic core in all its glory. Invisible shields filtered the dazzling snowstorm of stars. Burst of energy flashed as stars tore through the accretion disk in their hasty orbits, risking at every close encounter the infinite death that is contact with a black hole.

Or so Karramana enjoyed imagining it. As they knew from their studies, this stable, slow-spinning core harbored a company of well-behaved stars that followed predictable courses and never plunged through the event horizon. Well, hardly ever.

At last, though, even Karramana tired of staring at the infinite wonder of ten million stars knitting their light around the darkest object in the universe. There were too many ideas knitting themselves together inside their head — ideas that needed to be shared. They kicked off one more time, angling to the railing and taking hold beside the law-man.

"Caretaker has given me a wonderful idea of what to do now, Director Schoonover."

"Who?" He wanted to be called Calum, they remembered.

"Sorry, Calum."

"No, that's all right. Who had a wonderful idea?"

"You know. Caretaker. The one who takes care of the station and lives in the Quadrant of Light."

"Oh," he said, and his expression changed a few times before settling into something they saw as almost amusement. "I hope your mother doesn't decide to leave right away. I'd like to hear more about Caretaker."

"Oh, yes," they told him. "My idea means that we would stay here, like Caretaker has stayed here, to take care of things."

"What would we take care of?" he wanted to know.

They didn't want to correct him, that he'd said *we* instead of *you*. They liked the idea he would be part of their project.

Karramana leaned over the railing, to see if Mother was listening. She seemed distracted, but noticed Karramana looking at her.

"Yes, Karramana, what would ... we ... take care of?"

"We would take care of animals, the precious animals that are very rare, and we would make a place for people to come and see them and teach the people about them. It would be like nothing else, ever, a brand-new thing."

"Well, now —" Mother began.

Calum waved his fingers in that little movement that meant *tell me more*. "There's never been anything like that at the Truck Stop. What would you call it?"

"The Place for Precious Animals," they announced.

"That's kind of a long name. For advertising, we're going to need something a little catchier."

"Advertising?"

His lips curled and she saw his little white human teeth gleaming under the Dome. "Yes, we'll have to advertise widely, to tell people there's more to do here than eating and drinking and — well, other things. How do you like this name: The Truck Stop Zoo?"

"Zoo?"

"It's short for Zoological Garden, a sanctuary for animals."

"Sanctuary means a safe place, right?"

Calum nodded.

"I like that." Karramana decided. "So let's call it the Zoological Sanctuary. Gardens are for plants."

Calum's smile changed, and he made that snorting sound humans do when they are trying not to laugh. "I know. You can sell souvenirs. You could print out models of the animals."

"Yes," Karramana said. "And we'll have gift bags for people to take home that will have the name on it, like my bag from the gift shop."

They thought about the fun things they'd bought in the gift shop yesterday. The little yippy creature, they couldn't feel interested in it anymore, but the station model that Mother had said was too advanced for Boy, well, it would be easy for Karramana.

Calum suddenly frowned and turned to Mother. "Is this all right with you?" He said it in a strangely sad tone, like maybe he knew that she planned to go.

Karramana echoed that sadness, remembering Mother's plan to find a nice planet and settle there. "Please, Mama. Can we try? I know it's my fault Ashoka ran away —"

"It doesn't matter," Mother said. "Never mind. Everything's all right, Karramana. None of that matters anymore."

Karramana kicked off again and sailed across the dome under the starlight. Their attachment to Mother shimmered like a tracing of a star's orbit. Their attachment to Ashoka — still safely inside their skinsuit — glowed close to their own hearts. The connection with Caretaker made a sparkly filament that twirled overhead as the station turned. Down there at the railing, a bright bond glimmered between Mama and Calum.

It didn't matter that the client had run away and they had failed the contract.

The two wandering Darroughons had a place to be, now.

This place had given them new friends, new attachments.

This would be the place they would stay, together, forever and ever.

EPILOGUE

T HERE ARE CERTAIN QUESTIONS that most visitors want to ask the Director of the Truck Stop's Zoological Sanctuary, but they don't, for fear of seeming foolish. Children ask those questions, because children, no matter the species, tend to be forthright.

Many visitors have heard, though they usually do not mention the idea on-station, that the proprietors of the zoo are not really human. It may be nothing but a story, but it is a more interesting story than that of a single mother setting up shop at the truck stop with her precocious child. This story goes that the owners are some kind of advanced — or, in some renditions, terribly dangerous and horrifying — aliens who prefer to disguise themselves as humanoids, to better fit in with the general population in this busiest sector of the station.

When challenged on this, the senior proprietor, known as Deralka, is fond of saying, "Human is as human does."

She is gracious and meticulous, and extremely technologically savvy. No one has ever succeeded in an attempt to skim funds from the operation's accounts, and her security systems protect the animals even from well-meaning attempts to feed them unapproved foods. She travels widely, researching new additions to the zoo or acquiring supplies to improve the lives of the rare and endangered creatures they have rescued.

Her partner, the director, who conducts tours and manages the day-to-day facility operations, has a way of speaking to those who attempt to skirt rules during tours. It is a way of speaking that says, 'Hurt my animals, and you may discover what it is to be hurt.'

The animals here are the most fascinating anywhere. The guide will let you touch certain of the creatures, while thrilling you with the calm statement, "Keep in mind. Animals feel. And if you hurt an animal, you have given it permission to hurt you back."

There will always be one who says, with just a touch of fear, "Will it bite me?"

The guide will say, "Look. Does this animal have teeth?"

All the heads in the circle of admirers will bob or weave or whatever gesture means agreement.

"Well, then," the guide says. "If it has teeth, it may bite. If you threaten it, then it has the *right* to bite you." To be certain the sense of danger doesn't wither away in some platitude, the attendees are then told, "Don't worry, we have an emergency surgeon here in Green Quadrant."

Many an adult visitor has run to Security with complaints about the zoo staff's views on animal rights. Clever complainants may see the holo image of the security chief in the company of Deralka and choose to voice some other complaint or, if they notice that Deralka and the chief are holding hands in the image, they will instead deliver praise for the zoo and ask a simple question concerning their own travel authorizations.

Never has a child complained.

The star of the zoo is Ashoka, the famous cretzina that opened the way to communications, however brief and strange, with the mysterious entity inhabiting the Orange Quadrant. She will preen over her offspring, fuzzy balls of feathers and knives, and the guide will let each visitor make an introduction to Ashoka, with one finger — or equivalent organ — passed ever so gently through the topmost feathery hairs that Ashoka raises up for petting. No one has ever been bitten by Ashoka.

One visitor did have a hole drilled through his hand, but he deserved it.

Usually, it is during the visit with Ashoka that the children ask those special questions.

The first is always, "What's your name?"

The answer will be laughter, followed by, "You forget so easily. I told you my name at the start. Please learn to pay attention. It is an important life skill."

If one is lucky, one will hear the less-often-asked, "Is that your own hair?" The guide has long, curly hair the color of rainbows, though these space-born children would likely describe it as the color of a visible-light spectrum. One should be aware that the range of "visible" varies, and that the rainbow hair has streaks of silver that some may see as pastel streamers of infrared or ultraviolet hues.

"Well, I paid for the mods from my very own earnings, so yes, this hair is all my very own."

The guide's face, within the rainbow frame, has a certain androgyny that either confuses or disturbs adults, while it universally draws children closer.

Inevitably, one of the young ones will ask, "Are you a boy or a girl?"

They make a most attractive smile, this Darroughon wrapped in a custom-designed skinsuit that scattered rumors make out to be something other than a humanoid person. "What a silly question. There is only one of me, just like there is only one of each of you. Maybe I am a girl, and maybe I am a boy, but probably I am something else. I am Karramana. I am myself."

AUTHOR'S NOTE

Seeds for *The Smugglers* were planted several ago. I wanted to tell the story of an adventurous child and their mother, inspired by a young child I met at a science-fiction convention. This kid was smart, full of self-confidence, and shared my delight in collecting badge ribbons. I'd brought all my possible shares, and they sorted through the set and selected what I agreed were the very best ones ... under the bemused eye of a mother who knew what a treasure she had and was both prepared to protect — when necessary — and supportive of the new experiences her offspring was gathering. Of course, I can't be specific, but if they should happen upon this story, well, I hope they like it.

For all the SFF-loving kids out there, and the grown-ups who nurture them (and read the same books), I did not hold back on vocabulary or science or the tropes we love, like getting lost in a giant alien-built space structure. I trust them to trust me to not talk down to them; they probably know more about all of these things than I do. It's their territory I'm building stories in, and I'm grateful for being allowed to play.

It takes a community to make a story happen. The formation of the Truck Stop at the Center of the Galaxy group gave me a setting for this one, and I relied on Bob Schoonover's and Steve Soult's design of the Station and their tolerance of my kibitzing and what-ifs. We won't mention Steven Radecki's cat-herding, which advanced the project from pie-in-the-sky to ancient-ship-in-orbit.

The East Bay Science Fiction and Fantasy Writers provided a forum for the story to receive critique from a variety of readers, and I'm immensely grateful to all who took part. I'd like to give special shout-outs to two members of that group: M Verant and Sibyl Saint. Mike gave the piece his usual close read and story arc coverage. Sibyl went above and beyond, catching where I'd skipped over a truly crucial scene and encouraging me to expand the novel to open with the child's point of view, incorporate more details about the Truck Stop, and inject the sense of wonder any of us would have on arriving at this most wonderful place — the center of our home galaxy.

I also need to acknowledge the regulars of the South Bay Writers Club open mics, who took this whole journey with Karramana and their mother, from start to finish, through months of ten-minute readings. Thanks are due to William Albert Baldwin, Carolyn Donnell, Dave M. Strom, Alice Wu, and our varied cast of fellow storytellers. There's nothing like reading a work-in-progress aloud to find the spots that need improving — and build confidence by discovering the passages that touch listeners.

Of course, my family (especially my husband, Alan Wray) put up with my overworking, overtalking, and under-housekeeping this whole time and spared encouraging words when they weren't cooking meals, shopping, or doing chores that probably I should have been taking care of.

Thank you all.

ABOUT THE AUTHOR

Vanessa MacLaren-Wray writes speculative fiction for adults, children, and in-betweens, exploring the challenges of communication and attachment in a diverse, complex universe. As a mechanical engineer, her work has supported shifting to new energy technologies, especially renewables and storage. She also likes to build oddball robots who brew tea and play music.

Although denying any knowledge of alien technologies or extrasolar civilizations, when asked to write what she knows, Vanessa gravitates towards wormhole-based transit systems and cultural matrices only partly occupied by human beings.

Vanessa is the author of *All That Was Asked*, *Coke Machine*, and *Parrish Blue*. You can find all her work, including her website, *Cometary Tales*, and ongoing email journal, *Messages from the Oort Cloud*, through her master link: *https://linktr.ee/Vanessa_MacLarenWray*.

ALSO BY THE AUTHOR

All That Was Asked

by Vanessa MacLaren-Wray

It was supposed to be an easy jaunt to observe the stick-like aliens of Deep Valley Universe.

Parrish Blue

by Vanessa MacLaren-Wray

Sallie never expected to discover a world she'd forgotten how to imagine.

ALSO IN THIS SERIES

THE STARGAZER GIFT SHOP

by Steve Soult

What would you buy at the Stargazer Gift Shop at the center of the galaxy?

COKE MACHINE

by Vanessa MacLaren-Wray

Every truck stop needs a coke machine.

HIPPOLYTA'S DAGGER

by L. A. Jacob

Someone's always watching.